SLASH AND TURN

A Jaden Steele Carmel Mystery

Barbara Chamberlain

Barbara Chamberlain

Cups of Gold Publishing
Los Gatos, California

The Jaden Steele Carmel Mystery Series
A Slice of Carmel
Slash and Turn

First North American Edition
Copyright 2012 Barbara Chamberlain

1. Mystery and Detective Stories. 2. Ballet-Fiction.
3. Knives-Fiction. 4. Monterey, California-Fiction.
5. Carmel, California-Fiction. 6. Jaden Steele
(Fictitious character.)

ISBN 978-1479378081

Cover art by Elizabeth A. Miklavcic
www.anotherlanguage.org

www.jadensteelemysteries.com

To Beth and Jimmy Miklavcic of Another Language Performing Arts Company for the beautiful cover designs and formatting help with The Jaden Steele Carmel Mystery Series www.anotherlanguage.org

Sometimes you want something so much that you will do anything to have your own way. Though you might suspect an evil purpose, your desire engulfs your better judgment just as the ocean waves engulf everything in their path.

You are adrift in a cold ocean dusted with fog when you see color in the mist, a tropical island filled with your desire. Which wave do you want to ride in to the lustrous white sand?

Love? Money? Power?

But it is a mirage that disappears when you come near. Like the end of the rainbow, the warm beach is always somewhere else.

--Barbara Chamberlain

The sharp blade bit into her thumb. To her surprise, for a few seconds, it did not hurt. When the flash of pain hit, her hand began to shake. She felt the warm blood and dug into her purse for a handkerchief. The white cloth turned pink as she pressed it on the oozing knife jab. Certain that none of the company had noticed her, she dove into the alleyway and shoved the knife quickly into the hands of the person in the shadows. How could anything so lovely be so dangerous? Without a word she whirled, running to the small bus that would take them on a sightseeing tour to the remote Big Sur on the Central Coast of California.

She had stolen the blade only because of that promise. Would the promise be kept?

Her stomach muscles clenched at the fear of betrayal. The doubt hurt more than her finger. On the way down to Big Sur she tried to hide her trembling hand by keeping it in her pocket. The Carmel cutlery shop owner, Jaden Steele, had told them about the Gideon knives. They were sharp enough to cut through small bones.

I should have been more careful.

She shivered.

Their stage manager, Nicolas, turned backward in his seat to ask in Russian, "Do you feel all right? You look so pale."

Edward Stennis, their American guide, who spoke Russian very well, heard the question, and also looked back at her curiously for a second. She closed her eyes to slits but could still see his face. As the driver he had to turn back immediately to keep his eyes focused on the road. He was a fit man with muscular shoulders, a trim waist, and no wrinkles. She thought only his white hair betrayed him as older.

He carried himself tall, erect, almost like a dancer. No. Maybe military. The thought made her heart race. Her parents always feared the military in the old Soviet Union. Did the Americans spy on all the tourists as happened in many countries?

2

Edward turned on the microphone to described the area they were passing.

Point Lobos. He explained that Lobos was the Spanish word for wolves. "It is said that Robert Louis Stevenson modeled descriptions in his book, *Treasure Island*, after this area. Though he was not well for all of his life, he traveled from Scotland to Monterey to propose to his true love, Fanny Van de Grift Osbourne. The journey almost killed him. Some ranchers nursed him until Fanny and her son, Lloyd, came to help."

She stared out the window, barely aware of his words because of the wild ocean and the rugged cliffs that gave her the idea that they were at the edge of forever. "I am fine, Nicolas. Just tired. I'll close my eyes for a few minutes. I will be better." In her half-awake state, she thought, Point Lobos. *In this world, you are either a wolf or its prey.*

When her eyes closed, everything turned as red as the blood that came from her finger, as red as the smooth, comfortable handle of the knife that she had stolen.

In about five minutes her eyes popped open. The bleeding had stopped. She kept her index finger pressed tightly against the handkerchief wrapped thumb. Everyone was talking about the haunting Big Sur scenery, their visit to the California Art Gallery, the cutlery store, and the delicious luncheon at The Mad Hatter's bistro in Dolores Court.

"Fresh strawberries in winter," someone, maybe Tatiana, was saying, "Strawberries and honeydew melon, just for decoration next to the sandwich. Did you ever taste anything so fresh and delicious?"

Her finger stung. She wished she had stayed at the hotel with those who wanted to rest. Regret made her head pound.

Guilt pressed on her aching head like a heavy rock. She had stolen because she wanted to stay in the United States. She would not be able to dance forever.

Careful to keep his eyes on the road, Edward spoke softly to his mother who was in the first passenger seat right behind him, "Did you ever think a month ago that we would be taking two of the most famous ballet stars in the world sightseeing? Frederic Melnikov and Tatiana Myrakova? Don't you wish you had some of their energy? Don't you wish you were the age of these dancers again? That Frederic already asked me about Jaden. 'Does she have a friend?' I told him she has several," he whispered to his mother,

" I wish I were thirty years younger."

She turned to smile at him. "You finally realized that the most precious thing in life

4

is time. The richest and most powerful can't buy it."

Edward sighed. No use going into philosophy with mom. She was too sharp. He changed the subject. "They're having a good time. Except the pale one. If she is getting sick, I hope she warns us."

Esther Stennis nodded.

"Mom, why don't you tell them something about the area? Maybe the Big Sur Marathon." He handed her the mike.

Esther began, "Ten miles back we left the finishing area for the famous Big Sur Marathon. The end of our drive will be at the beginning of the run, twenty-six miles of scenery that you won't forget. Most of the marathon is uphill. Remarkably, the winners finish in about two hours…."

"When is the race run?" asked Frederic Melnikov, certainly the most well-known of their passengers. Notorious, actually. Edward thought that Frederic knew he was famous but the man was not egotistical like some well-known celebrities he had met.

Esther responded, "The last weekend in April. Thousands of runners, walkers, and sightseers descend on Big Sur for the race."

Edward settled into his driver's seat, thinking back to noon when he and his mom met the company for lunch at The Mad Hatter's Café in Dolores Court. During lunch he watched Jaden Steele arranging a new display in the courtside window of her cutlery store. Several of the ballet company members were admiring her store and the Carmel beach seascape featured in the window of the California Art Gallery in the court directly opposite Jaden's. The interior court, protected from the constant street traffic, was ideal for leisure outdoor dining. Those who lived in the upstairs apartments, like his mother, had easy access downstairs to some of the best food in Carmel. Both of the owners were excellent chefs.

He knew his mother loved having him stay with her after all these years. He was home shopping in the Monterey Bay area with the idea that she could live with him. His mom liked living in the court. Now that he had stayed there for several months, he understood why. The location was convenient right in the middle of the town. She did not need a car. And the court residents treated her like family.

That morning he had finally decided to ask Jaden if he could bring the visitors into the store.

Everyone was almost finished eating. "Mom, I'm going to talk to Jaden about bringing the dance company members in for shopping. We have an hour before we are scheduled to do the tour. Be right back."

Jaden was concentrating intently on her display set-up. Although she was right next to the door, the bell startled her when he walked into the shop. Her deep blue-violet eyes widened in surprise and she smiled. Her contagious smile was one of her most attractive features. For the umpteenth time Edward suddenly wished again he was thirty years younger. Or, to be honest, would he want to relive his life?

The new store owner looked up from replacing her cutlery display in the picture window that faced the inside of Dolores Street Court. For this first Christmas in California, the owner of A Slice of Carmel had decided to show off the diamond bladed, special holiday edition of the Gideon knife line. This was the first time the handles had been manufactured in red and green, and they would be discontinued January 1. She felt collectors would be buying them. They contrasted vividly with the white angel hair she had placed between the ceramic houses that had belonged to her grandmother.

Although the café's five patio tables in the court were unusually crowded, no one had come into her store all morning. Though no action in the store was always disappointing, the quiet gave plenty of time to unpack the treasured houses. They made her feel so in touch with the spirit of her grandmother, Ethel Cooper. Jaden missed her grandparents. She was so young when her parents died that she had trouble remembering them.

Jaden really enjoyed arranging displays and loved buying the inventory.

She pressed the power strip. The lights in the houses glowed. The warm lights whisked her back to her childhood when she asked her grandmother who lived in the small houses, and why did they hide when Jaden wanted to see them?

"Don't little people live in the houses?"

"You are such a curious little girl, Jaden," Grandma Ethel answered. "And you have a wonderful imagination. Never lose that, love, no matter what happens. It's the greatest nation, im-a-gi-nation."

While she finished college, began teaching communication at the university, and her short four year marriage, Jaden's imagination was pushed to the back of her mind until she moved to Carmel. She was not an artist, like their neighbor, Bill, whose featured local scenes commanded $16,000 a canvas in the California Gallery. She was not a writer, like a number of authors who lived in the village. Right now she was using her imagination to publicize her business.

The ring of the brass bell tied to the door filled the shop.

Retired General Edward Stennis entered. "That display of lighted houses looks like the holidays have arrived in California, Jaden. And I've never seen those colors in the knife handles." His clear blue eyes, so much like his mother's, mirrored the movement of people in the crowded court.

"These are a special holiday edition, Edward. Someone in their marketing department decided to get into the holiday buying trade. Smart move, I think." Jaden touched the chimney of one of the colorful ceramic houses.

"When my grandmother set up the lighted houses they fascinated me. I loved them because I could imagine a warm, welcoming village. Christmas was coming. Those childhood memories stay with you always. When I moved from Nebraska, I could not give them away." She sighed, knowing she was monopolizing the conversation. "Edward, how is the house hunting? Found anything?"

"A difficult work in progress. I know my mother must be tired of me mooching off her upstairs. I've seen a lot of homes but not the *one*. At those outrageous prices I'm determined to find what I want or to build it. Jaden, today mom and I are tour guides."

"I didn't know you did tours," she said with a grin.

"Normally I don't but Mayor Rawlings put out a request for Russian speakers."

Jaden blinked. When General Stennis finally found his elusive house, it certainly would have to have some huge closets for his numerous skeletons.

Edward Stennis smiled in his most charming manner. He knew that Jaden's skeptical violet eyes could never hide anything, especially her burning curiosity.

She was not at all like their neighbor and friend Bobbi Jones, the notorious Roberta Jones-Schmidt, who could probably go on the world poker tour. The two women were unique individuals.

"The company members are having lunch in the court. Mom's with them."

"She speaks Russian, too?" At age eighty-seven, Esther was one of the most remarkable women Jaden thought she would ever meet. She knew that spying ran in the Stennis family. Her curiosity smoldered to know more about the mother and son.

"We were in a cold war with Russia for years. You are way too young."

"Edward, I'm thirty-three and I certainly know history. It was a frightening time. I loved President Reagan's line, 'Mr. Gorbachev, tear down this wall.' It was a perfect example of imagining what you want and it will come true. But you know that. You were a kid, but probably there, weren't you? How many languages do you speak?"

Edward decided that Jaden had some ESP. He had been there, translating. It was his first year out of training. After President Reagan's shooting, the security for him was doubled. In a typical D. C. intrigue Edward was assigned to a ghost unit watching the Secret Service. "Five, but I'm rusty with all of them. Mom and I have been practicing. She loves both ballet and modern dancing."

"Is it the Kurloff Ballet Company? I read about them coming for December."

"Yes, they are performing the Nutcracker until December 30th in the new Monterey Performing Arts Center. It's quite an honor for the area. Ninety per cent of the tickets are gone."

"I'd better call today about tickets. Bobbi and I really want to go."

"There's great news that I wanted to tell you before I drive some of the company down to Big Sur. You don't have to buy tickets. Mom and I have guest passes for eight. You, Bobbi, Amanda Perkins, the library director, Bill Amirkhanian, Kyle and Sydney are included."

Kyle Foster and Sydney Allingham were the chefs who ran the popular Mad Hatter's Café in the Court. Bill was a Carmel police officer as well as an outstanding artist.

"You've listed everyone who lives in the upstairs apartments."

"Except Von Otto in #6," Edward answered with a smile. "Hope I meet him some day. You will have to admit that he is the best of neighbors. Absolutely quiet. I doubt any of us would recognize him and I'm sure he wants it that way."

Jaden's dark eyebrows went up. If anyone knew the residents of Dolores Court, it was Edward. The retired general investigated all of them before he came here from Washington D.C. The murder of city councilman and gallery owner Sergio Panetti destroyed the peaceful image of the tourist village. Although the murderer was Sergio's business partner, Jaden always felt guilty about the killings. She felt that in some way her move to Carmel-by-the-Sea triggered the murders. Bill and Bobbi tried to assure her that sooner or later Vincent, Sergio's partner, would have snapped.

She desperately tried to mentally put it all in a locked box without much success.

Edward went on, "What I wanted to ask was could I bring some of the company in here? I realize you don't like crowds in the store. Mom and I will be with them."

"Oh, I'd love to meet the performers. And thank you for inviting us to go with you. Seeing the Nutcracker performed by the Kurloff Ballet will be a wonderful experience. I've never seen a ballet performed in a theater."

"It's opening night. We are also invited backstage before the performance and to the cast party afterwards. It's going to be at a beautiful home on Seventeen-Mile Drive.

They wanted to perform in the Monterey Bay area so they could also be tourists."

"Edward, how marvelous! Bobbi is going to be thrilled. Me, too. Thank you! But what about Gene Miller?" Gene ran the California Art Gallery in the court.

"Gene already has tickets and an invite to the party. He is on the board of the Monterey Dance Academy. All of the children who are dancing in the performance are from the academy."

"I didn't realize that Gene was on the board. Great. I would not want to leave him out of our party."

"My pleasure, my lady." He smiled in that charming way that must have impressed many women through the years. Although he was older, his white hair, smooth skin, and good physical condition made him an attractive man.

"Bring the company members into the store. Everything is in cases anyway."

"Several of them speak English well, but we will have to translate for others. And Jaden, some are prima donnas. The most famous are treated like rock stars are treated here. As a word of warning, I doubt that they will buy much. The knives certainly cannot be taken on the plane." He put his hand on the door lever. "Those with shopping money are probably saving it for

Levis anyway." The brass bell rang softly as he went into the court.

The phone rang. "Hello, Slice of Carmel. Oh, hi, Bobbi." Jaden could not wait to blurt out the news about the opening night tickets and party.

"Jaden, that's a dream come true! It was really a magnificent stroke to get the company to come to our area. I've been reading about them in the paper. Our social life is picking up."

"They are going to perform in San Jose and have been in Los Angeles and San Francisco. They've done other ballets. This is the only time they will do the Nutcracker in the States."

"Tell Edward super thanks for me. Are we still on for dinner?"

The door of A Slice of Carmel opened. Edward came in first followed by a small mob of people from the company.

"Bobbi, I'll have to hang up. The Russians are coming."

Edward introduced Jaden to the ballet company manager, Igor Kurloff.

"Welcome to Carmel, Mr. Kurloff."

He was a heavyset man, graying at the temples. He must have been handsome when he was young, but he was not aging well. "It is a pleasure to meet you. Edward tells me that you are the owner of this shop. What a magnificent display. And swords in these wall cases. Do you sell them?"

Since they were in wall cases without prices, it was a natural question.

"We sell about one a year."

"And this small knife in the case with the gold-handled sword. It is small and old. Not a sword." He pointed with a hand that was probably twice as large as hers.

"My grandfather made that knife. I followed him every minute when he made it from the blade to carving the bone for the handle. He ran a butcher shop in Kearny, Nebraska. All of his handles were polished white bone."

"And this is where you learned about knives to now run shop," he guessed.

About fifteen people crowded into the store, exclaiming in Russian over the goods. Jaden realized that at five feet seven she was taller than most of the visitors in the shop, but not anything close to the prime physical condition of the dancers. She was introduced to them one by one-Tanya, Nadia, Maria, Peter, Demetri, Sergey, George, *George!* and tried to remember the names until her head started swimming. She finally gave up. Nadia was limping because of an ankle sprain. She might not dance this week.

Dancing is stressful, like any strenuous activity, and dancers are easily injured. Their feet and joints can suffer permanent damage from the physical demands.

Edward was still introducing, "Jaden, this is the company's equipment manager, Nicolas Kurloff."

She decided that at least she could remember Kurloff. Nicolas and Igor must be brothers. They looked very much alike. Both were burly, more like football players. She would ask Edward about the relationship. As most of the company finished their lunches, the store became more and more packed. She tried to help as many as possible, and actually made a few sales. This was a day she could have used Hal's help, but the former owner of the store was on his honeymoon in Kauai. About half of the group looked like they wanted to purchase. All of them paid with cash. She guessed they did not have the money, or were waiting to find Levis, as Edward suggested. Jaden wondered how much a dancer in a Russian company made.

Tour guide Edward approached the counter with a slim, blonde woman about Jaden's height whom she recognized. The prima ballerina gazed at her with penetrating blue eyes flecked with black.

Edward said, "Jaden, this is Tatiana Myrakova. Jaden Steele."

"I am so pleased to meet you," Tatiana said with a charming accent as she took Jaden's hand. Her nails were long and glowed with deep crimson polish. Her grasp was firm, not like one would expect from such a graceful woman. Jaden was reminded that these ballet dancers were pure muscle. They trained from their childhood on and probably spent hours a day exercising.

"Miss Myrakova, it is an honor. I am so looking forward to your performance."

"Thank you. I have very much enjoyed my visit here. Edward says that you own this store. How marvelous. Have you much work? America is such an...open country."

"It's a lot of work, Miss Myrakova. And a lot of paperwork. Accounts."

"Yes. I understand. Capitalism is not easy. Please call me Tatiana. This knife," she pointed to a Gideon in the display case, "is in the window. The blade is not steel? The handle color is so unusual."

"The red and green handles are a special edition for the holiday season. The blade is called ceramic. Actually the material is man-made diamond, zirconium oxide. The secret process makes it second in hardness only to diamonds. They rarely need sharpening."

"Really?" Tatiana's perfectly arched dark eyebrows rose.

"The blade is dangerous. I warn people to only take it by the handle, never the blade. One could easily slice off a whole finger with a Gideon blade."

Igor appeared at the dancer's side. "My dear, it is time to leave." He placed one hand on her shoulder. Jaden noticed that she flinched. He drew back his hand. "Tatiana, Edward and his mother, Esther, are taking us to Carmel Mission and down Highway One to Big Sur next. We hear it is most beautiful coastlines in California."

A frown wrinkled Tatiana's forehead.

Jaden thought she forced the frown away and nodded solemnly. Sometimes she wished she were not so observant. Details annoyingly stuck with her.

"The scenery is spectacular. I have not been there. I'm planning to visit a well-known historic home down there in January. The family has advertised a sword that belonged to a famous person in California history, Captain Josiah Bartlett."

"How interesting," Tatiana said as she stared out the large glass window, looking at something that was not there.

If it were the cold war era, Jaden might have taken Igor for a KGB agent. The Kurloffs were older, probably sixtyish.

Agents tried to protect their famous dancers from defecting to the west. That was the era when Edward Stennis, and probably his mother, were in the secret agent game.

Edward moved up to the counter with another dancer that Jaden immediately recognized. Frederic Melnikov danced the part of the Nutcracker. He was famous in America for often being photographed dating starlets and other women-in-the-news. Women adored the ballet star. She remembered reading an interview with him,

"Frederic is not a name used in Russia. My mother, who was a ballerina with the Kiev ballet and also a teacher, watched many American movies. She loved Fred Astaire's dancing in the motion pictures and decided to name me after him. She knew I would be a dancer because I would move the most in her womb when Fred was on screen. I loved his dancing, too, always with beautiful, graceful women. My mother would say, 'Look at him, Frederic. He is romance on film.' The man really could not sing and he was not a great actor. But when he danced he captured the whole black and white screen."

Movies often were the only impression other countries had of the United States. When she and her husband, Brent, took their one tour out of the country, it was to the beautiful fiords of Norway. Many of the people asked if they knew any cowboys. Brent answered, "Sure! We know Tom Mix, Roy Rogers, Gene Autry, Randolph Scott...." He went on with any cowboy star he could remember from television reruns of old movies. He left the Norwegians open-mouthed. Her husband had a rare sense of humor that she missed. Kyle Foster had a good sense of humor and so did Hal, the former owner of her cutlery shop.

She did not think of Brent as often now, but when she did that pang of loneliness still struck like a knife jab. Since his death four years earlier, she had been with one man, charming Sergio Panetti, who was a womanizer and was murdered because of it. Jaden felt like a complete fool when she learned he was married. She vowed never to repeat that mistake. Being lonely is no excuse for losing one's common sense.

Frederic Melnikov smiled broadly and bowed. Frederic's hair was dyed an unusual brilliant, unnatural reddish color. His body was all muscle. Like Tatiana, he had a perfect ballet dancer's body. They moved with such grace, even when shopping in a store. His dark eyes twinkled with a smile, and he said, "How do you do, Mrs. Steele? You have a marvelous store. And you are the owner?"

Jaden answered, "Yes. It is a pleasure to meet you. I have admired your dancing and the company's performances on television."

Frederic smiled broadly. "You follow ballet? You do look like you are interested in many things."

Jaden had to smile thinking that no wonder Frederic was a media darling. His physique was magnificent. No fat. Pure muscle. She thought he was interested in many things, too--mostly women. Jaden felt embarrassed that she was immediately attracted to his natural charm. "Yes. And modern dance and tap dancing. Most forms of the dance."

"I learned tap dancing from watching movies. Many people are surprised by that."

"You must be a wonderful tap dancer."

"Thank you," Frederic answered with a broad smile. His brown eyes glistened. "I often think of the times my mother and I watched Fred Astaire in the movies-every one of his films. Top Hat with his wonderful partner Ginger Rogers. The number Cheek to Cheek. I know it by heart. Movement by movement. How proud my mother would be of me now." He cleared his throat. "I am sorry. She is gone. Died many years back."

"I'm sorry for your loss," Jaden told him sincerely. "My parents died when I was six years old. When those close to us die, a part of us misses them forever. There's an empty spot where they should be."

"You have a very kind nature, Jaden Steele. I hope to see you again soon. We are leaving on a sightseeing trip now to the coast below Carmel, Big Sur. You are coming to a performance?"

"Yes, Edward has invited us to the opening night and to a cast party. We are delighted to be included. Since the new theater is not very large, we feel privileged."

"We? Your husband?"

"No, I am a widow."

"Please accept my sorrow at your loss."

"Thank you. It's been four years."

The dancer's face stayed sympathetic. "As you say, part of us misses dear ones forever. When they are loved, they are always part of our pleasant memories."

His instincts are so sharp. He has a talent for a lot more than dancing. "Edward has invited the six of us who live in the apartments upstairs. When I bought this business, the owner offered me his apartment. It's very convenient."

"How delightful. You have a flat upstairs close to your business. Your own flat." Frederic said with a brilliant smile. No wonder the tabloids loved photographing the famous dancer.

Jaden wondered how many women the popular dancer had conquered with his smile. Too many, she imagined. As attractive as Frederic was, he began to remind her of Sergio, her murdered ex-lover. Thinking of that man always made her feel like a fool. But she sensed Frederic was not really like him. The dancer struck her as open and honest. If he had a wife somewhere he would say so.

I need to pay attention to some of the others in the store.

Edward must have noticed because he came over to the counter with a vaguely familiar woman who had rich chestnut hair and hazel eyes. She was about three inches shorter than Jaden's five foot seven inches.

"Jaden, before we left I wanted to introduce you to Maria Essipov. Igor wants the company members who are here to go to the bus now to continue the tour of the area down to Big Sur."

"I am so very glad to meet you." Maria extended her hand to Jaden.

"And I you, Miss Essipov. I hope you are enjoying your visit to Carmel. Frederic was just telling me that he loves tap dancing from watching American movies."

Maria commented with a pleasant smile, "Frederic is...is" her eyes rolled toward the ceiling. "I do not know English word. He does many things. I do ballet."

"Really? How interesting. Have you thought of Broadway, Frederic?" Edward took his elbow to gently steer him toward the door. "Do you have an agent?"

The famous dancer did not resist the obvious effort to take him out of the store. He said to Jaden, "I will be looking forward to seeing you again soon, Jaden Steele." She knew he was sincere.

Esther stopped by the counter. "Thank you for letting us mob the store like this. They can't get over the goods available in stores here. I like your Christmas display, and those red and green Gideons are elegant. The tree in the window that faces Sixth Street makes everything festive. How is the store doing, Jaden?"

"Just fine. Business has been great since the day after Thanksgiving. I would love to hear how and why you learned Russian."

Esther grinned. "One of these days. I was going to write a book, from the OSS to the Cold War, but Edward will have to publish it long after I'm gone." She rolled her sky blue eyes. "Rules, you know. Oh, looks like Igor has everyone out to the bus so I'll be going. Edward is also the driver."

"A book about your life ought to be something to read, but we'd rather have you here. Goodbye, Esther. Have a nice tour." Jaden shook her head. She only made six sales from that group but her head was swimming. She needed coffee. Her knowledge of the inventory had been challenged today with all the people distracting her and asking for information. She felt that she had answered questions from the company members very well.

Her stomach was rumbling.

Chowder at The Mad Hatter's would be great. Jaden pulled the keys from her pocket and turned the sign on the door to closed, moved the hands of the paper clock to "Return at two p.m." and went out to the court. This was a common practice in Carmel where many of the small shops had only one or two employees. Lowering overhead was often the only way a business could stay alive.

Enrique Ruiz, the busboy/waiter/court handyman was just cleaning two tables when she approached a table. He wiped his hands on the sides of his apron, which was printed with those famous scenes from Lewis Carroll's *Mad Hatter's Tea Party.*

Kyle told her about loving the tea party scene from the classic book because it reminded him of his own out-of-the-ordinary life. To him it seemed the perfect choice for a name for the café.

"This one is ready, Misses Jaden." Enrique held the chair for her.

Kyle had trained him well. "Thank you, Enrique. You were busy."

"Yes. Those customers good eaters. They ate everything on the plates. Even parsley. Mira. Look at that."

Jaden surveyed the cleaned plates and nodded her head. "They were good eaters. They are mostly dancers, Enrique. They need lots of energy." She sat down. "Enrique, I would like clam chowder, French bread, and coffee, please."

"You have it, Misses Jaden," Enrique smiled and moved quickly toward the café entrance. The Mad Hatter's had a large kitchen set up perfectly for catering. There was only a small four table area inside for customers. Most people preferred to eat under the royal blue market umbrellas in the court that was insulated from the traffic.

Kyle Foster, one of the café's owners, came over to her table. "Jaden, did you get your invitation from Edward? Isn't it wonderful to go to an opening night? And to see Melnikov in person. He achieves such remarkable elevation on his jumps."

"We are really lucky. I love the ballet."

Enrique appeared with a small coffee carafe and a mug for her. He poured the steaming liquid into the mug and smiled. "No sugar. No cream."

"Good memory. Thank you, Enrique. How are the classes coming?" She knew he was taking English classes at Monterey Peninsula College.

"Excellent," Enrique said. "December fifteenth we have Christmas break."

"He is a first class waiter," Kyle told her as Enrique returned to cleaning off one of the other tables. "I hope he never realizes how much he could get working at one of the expensive restaurants in the village."

"He'll catch on soon enough."

Kyle sighed. "I know. Right now he gets excited about a four dollar tip. It was wonderful to meet Tatiana Kurloff and Frederic Melnikov. Such an honor to meet such famous dancers and most of the rest of the company. We took pictures for the newspapers and television."

"Tatiana Kurloff? She is a Kurloff, too?"

"Married to Igor. Didn't you know that? Well, why should you? She uses her maiden name for professional reasons, or personal ones. I don't know. Rumors say they lead separate lives."

"I would never have thought of them as a married couple." Jaden took a sip of the steaming coffee. "Your coffee is always great, Kyle." She thought that Tatiana behaved as though she did not even like Igor. Jaden hesitated to say that to Kyle. She thought men are worse gossips than women, although they will not admit it.

"Thank you. Our coffee is our trade secret. You are the only one we ever gave our special blend of whole beans. You are at the top of our preferred list," Kyle's beautiful smile put her at ease.

Enrique returned with the hot chowder and French bread. "Enjoy," he said.

"There's probably no better meal than this in Carmel. Sydney has a secret for his chowder, too." Although she knew better than to add the calories, somehow the butter leapt onto the knife and onto the hot bread. "I think I like this bread better than dessert." Enjoyment banished her guilt.

The tall, thin café owner smiled at her. "Thank you. I like your window scene, Jaden. The dancers were admiring your window and Bill's painting in the window of Gene Miller's Gallery. Frederic Melnikov said that he loved that painting. Gene was trying his best to make a sale. Even a dancer as famous as Melnikov probably could not afford that price. Jaden, I must compliment you on your clever knife display. Those red and green handles are beautifully curved."

"They are very comfortable to hold, too," Jaden told him.

"We love our own set, even though it is the older white bladed style. They are so sharp we keep them on a high shelf. Only Sydney uses them."

Jaden glanced up quickly, her eyes narrowing. Her voice deserted her completely. In a few seconds she managed to get control of herself and the terrifying memories that followed after Kyle and Sydney earned their ceramic knife set.

"I'm sorry." His face flushed. Kyle and Sydney received the set of knives in payment for catering the new ownership party when she took over the store. At that party she met Sergio's wife. The memory made her clench her teeth. He begged her to meet him at midnight and explain. That moment of shock would never leave her. She never had the chance to tell him that they were finished. He was stabbed that night in the parking garage below the court. Jaden never told anyone, even Bobbi, that finding the murdered Sergio was less of a shock than learning he was married.

Something warm and furry rubbed against her leg. She reached down to pet the huge white cat, Arizona, that Kyle and Sydney had rescued after a flood in that state and given to Esther Stennis. Through the Salvation Army, Kyle and Sydney took a kitchen van to disasters. They were busy for two weeks during the last Big Sur fire.

Arizona usually sat sphinx-like on the post at the top of the stairs.

Jaden tried to keep the terror of discovering the murder in the back of her mind. Often the memories snaked their way forward. Because they were both suspects in the stabbing, she and Bobbi investigated the crime and found they were a good team. The librarian's past made her the first suspect. Jaden's relationship with the murdered man made her the second. Between the two of them they finally trapped one of two killers.

If it had not been for Bobbi's help, Jaden would not be alive today.

She stood up to watch three seagulls coasting toward Carmel beach. Jaden took a deep breath of the sea air and returned to work, pausing to admire her new window display. For a few brief seconds she was transported back to her grandparents' home in Nebraska. They raised her after her parents died. They were wonderful and she knew she was loved. At Christmastime grandfather set up her father's train set surrounded by the ceramic houses. She never tired of watching the train rattle down the miniature tracks.

Even minus Grandfather's train set the lighted houses did look nice with white angel hair between them. Those red and green handled knives fit right in to the season. *Who would buy a knife for a Christmas present? Hopefully a lot of people would be attracted by the colors.*

She blinked and pressed closer to the window. She stared through the plate glass into the display. One spot where she thought she had placed a knife was only plain white, silky angel hair.

A knife was missing.

Missing screamed at her from the other side of the glass.

For a few seconds Jaden paced back and forth in front of the window.

She stared through the plate glass that reflected the tables, chairs, and umbrellas.

The smallest Gideon knife on the end closest to the door was gone.

She fumbled with the key in the lock.

Once inside she reached into the angel hair. Only the ballet company members, Edward, and his mother, Esther, had visited the store all morning.

Jaden knew she remembered the placement of the knife. She felt around in the other knives. *Gone.* It was not there. She checked the display case by the computer. The only knives left in the drawer at the bottom of the display case were in boxes. The Gideon storage area of the glass shelf was empty. "I know I put the set of five of the holiday knives in the window." She walked to the window and counted the knives. Four. Jaden's hands felt the prickly angel hair one more time. That three inch red-handled paring knife was missing.

Deeply disappointed and hurt, she walked slowly to the desk, muttering, "I can't believe it, but one of the dance company must have taken that knife!" The loss of the sixty dollars was nothing compared to the sick feeling churning in her stomach. What should she do about what was certainly a theft?

The bell on the door rang again. Jaden looked up to see Carmel Police Sergeant Bill Amirkhanian come into the shop. "Afternoon, Jaden. Your tree in the window looks great on the street side."

"Hello, Bill," she answered flatly.

"Don't be so enthusiastic. I certainly was hoping you would be glad to see me. You look like you lost your best friend. What's wrong? Can I help with something?"

A frown set into his forehead.

She peered into those dark, dark eyes that always seemed to understand too much.

"You can, Bill. I was just trying to decide what to do. Having a police officer walk into the store must be a sign. Someone took a knife from the window display."

"I am at your service," He bowed and smiled. "Police officer in the flesh. First, are you certain it's missing? Could it have been dropped or moved? The red and green handles should be easy to spot."

"There's the empty space in the display case right in the corner next to the door. I searched the display window. None were sold. And Bill, I know all five of the set were in the display."

"You just have a twelve inch high barrier here to block off the display area. Really easy to reach over. The spot where you put the knife is right by the barrier. You should have someone build a door so it would have to be opened to reach the display. Let's search the floor."

They went over the floor inch by inch, the waste paper baskets and the bathroom.

The realization that one of the talented dancers would steal a knife made her pound the top of the display case in frustration. "It's gone! Bill, what am I going to do?"

"Report it stolen, of course."

"By someone in one of Russia's most famous ballet companies?"

"You won't be accusing anyone. Someone shoplifted a knife. Report it."

"You're right. Bill, I'm just so disappointed. Crowds in the store aren't safe, no matter if they include world famous dancers. You can't watch everyone, but those performers are so well-known."

"They are people. Most are very honest but there are a few bad ones. Those are the ones who take up our time. It's hard for me to remember ninety-five per cent of people are good when you only work with lawbreakers."

"All right. It won't be in the papers?"

"It may get into the printed crime reports in the Carmel News. Not major stuff. All you have to say is that someone stole a knife from your shop. You can't prove anything else right now."

"You're right, of course. I'm sure it was one of them. No one else was in the store this morning, except for Edward and Esther Stennis who are their tour guides. Did you know that they speak Russian? Anyway, I know neither of them would take a knife."

"Jaden, nothing surprises me anymore." He placed his hand on hers. "Besides, we really don't know Edward. He's retired military. I can guarantee you that he knows how to use a knife."

"He often admires the swords." She sighed deeply, thinking of how right he was about people, how Sergio Panetti's wife went totally crazy and changed into a murderess. Jaden's forearms bore the small scars of Marian's madness. The woman was in a mental hospital in Northern California.

I hope she stays there forever.

Bill's hand felt warm and comforting. She made herself pull her own away.

The tall man frowned slightly but made no move to touch her again. "Describe the knife to me and I'll make a report."

"It was red. Red handle. White blade. Three and a half inches long. Retails for $59.95 plus tax."

Bill gave a low whistle. "Sixty dollars for a three inch? Do you sell many?"

"Yes. They are very popular. They almost never need sharpening. And for someone whose paintings sell for $16,000, you should not be surprised."

"Touché But I don't get all of that money. The gallery takes forty per cent."

"That much? Well, I can't talk. But our mark-up is less than that."

"Gene Miller wanted fifty, but I told him I would try some of the other galleries." He pointed across the way where his painting of the Carmel River Beach took up the entire display window. A brass plaque under the oil declared, "Exclusive dealer for paintings by Aram."

Although she never told Bill, Jaden took a minute every day to admire the painting. Gene, the owner and its sole employee, caught her admiring it one day and, like a good salesman, offered to sell the river scene to her on time payments. Since she was making just a little over her expenses now, a purchase like that would be a foolish. She treasured the tiny painting Bill had given her and kept the oil on the nightstand by her bed. When he showed the miniature to Gene, the art expert told her it was valuable because Aram always worked in the large three by five foot canvas.

"Getting an exclusive on your work is a coup for Gene. He knows it. And, the artist lives right upstairs. What could be better?"

William Aram Amirkhanian smiled. He knew he loved Jaden. His senses warned him not to press her. He did not want to frighten her or drive her away. Bill knew he already had competition from attorney McKenzie Anderson, who fortunately lived in San Diego. Instead he asked, "Would you like to go out to dinner tonight? Maybe on the wharf? The lights on the boats are beautiful at night. Some of them are decorated for Christmas. Then we could drive into Pacific Grove and see the Christmas lights down Lighthouse Avenue."

"Bill, I'm sorry. Bobbi and I are going out tonight." She saw the smile vanish and said, "Could I have a rain check? Maybe Friday night?"

He shook his head. "Friday night I have the three to midnight duty."

"Saturday night is the ballet opening. You can come to that?"

"Yes, I traded with Roy. That means I have his evening shift on Sunday. Monday and Wednesday are my regular nights."

"All right. We have a date on Thursday next week," Jaden said, happy that the returned smile made his dark eyes sparkle. She warned herself to watch out because she liked him very much, more than anyone since her husband, Brent, had died. Brent was like her best friend. Her lawyer, McKenzie Anderson was a man like Brent. Bill was different. She was afraid of her feelings for him in a way that at first had mystified her.

Finally she did understand that she was really attracted to him. *Be careful*, a nagging voice in her head spoke.

"Thursday next week," he said with a nod. "I'm going to write out a theft report for you to sign, Jaden. May I use your computer? The forms are online and I can print one out."

The bell on the door rang to announce three tourists entering the store.

"Carmel is decorated so beautifully for Christmas," one woman commented.

"Those lights down the center of Ocean Avenue make everything look so festive," the other woman said. "I'm interested in the knives in the window. Can you tell me about them? I've never seen those handle colors."

The man with them asked, "Have you been to the Christmas symphony performance at the Carmel Mission? We're going tonight."

"The mission church is decorated with scarlet poinsettias for the symphony performances. They are striking on the whitewashed adobe walls. You are going to love it," Jaden told them, and began to describe the knives. "Those blades have a special additive. They are hot pressed and fired simultaneously, making them second in hardness to diamonds. This is a special holiday edition." She must say that five times a day. "Would you like to hold one?"

She took out a 4" knife from under the cabinet and placed it in the man's hand.

He commented, "It fits my hand perfectly. Very comfortable shape. Expensive," the man said when Jaden told them the prices. "but if they hold their edge ten times as long as any metal blade, we will try one."

Naturally they wanted the size that had been stolen. Jaden found two in boxes under the counter.

After they left, she commented, "When a customer holds something they buy."

Bill commented, "You are a good salesperson. The owner should definitely hire you. Jaden, would you like to go to the symphony performance at the mission? I know it's beautiful."

She smiled and nodded.

"Great! I'll get tickets." His smile brightened the room.

In spite of herself and how she felt about the theft, Jaden smiled back.

Saturday, at six-thirty in the evening, Sydney Allingham pulled his old, elegant Navy blue Lincoln into the parking lot of the Monterey Auditorium near the wharf.

"Isn't it exciting?" Bobbi's golden-flecked, almond shaped eyes were glowing. "Did you know this was based on a story by Hoffman, The Nutcracker and the Mouse King?" She asked in her reference librarian's mode and went on,

"It's so rare to have a famous group perform here. That's one thing I miss about San Diego. Though Monterey does have a number of events, there's more excitement in big cities. McKenzie told me he is going to the San Diego Symphony performance tonight, or he would probably have come up here. Carmel does not even have a movie theater." She smoothed down the long skirt of her dark brown velvet dress.

Jaden knew that Bobbi received a call from McKenzie Anderson about once a week. There was a strong bond between the woman and the man who was her lawyer. After a sensational trial that captured front pages for months, and every other form of media, Bobbi was acquitted of second degree murder charges in the accidental death of her abusive husband.

"McKenzie called me about three weeks ago," Jaden said. "He says he may not come to stay in his condo in Monterey until the spring. He likes the weather down south."

"McKenzie is really a handsome, intelligent man," Amanda Perkins offered. Her black velvet dress and wrap looked terrific. Black looks great on some women but did not suit others, like Bobbi. Jaden was wearing her only evening dress, a simple, twelve-year-old black silk with a scoop neck and three-quarter length sleeves.

No doubt ninety-eight per cent of the women, and men, would be wearing black.

The brown velvet of Bobbi's gown was perfect for her skin and made the golden flecks in her hazel eyes glow. Jaden watched

Bobbi squeeze her eyes shut. Furrows appeared in her forehead. She could almost read Bobbi's thoughts. McKenzie's name would always remind the librarian of the sensational trial, the worst time of her life.

Jaden decided to change the subject.

"I've seen the Nutcracker danced on television. Never a live performance. When I was growing up, my grandmother loved to play the record of the Tchaikovsky music and I would listen to it for hours in the parlor. Sometimes we would dance around the room."

"I remember records!" Bobbi teased. "The library only gave them up about eight years ago."

Jaden was too lost in her pleasant memories to notice the teasing. "Yes. My grandparents had a record player. We listened to that record until it was scratched and jumped in several places. How I hated to sell that player when I sold their home, our home, to come out here."

"They raised you from the time you were very young, didn't they?" Bobbi asked.

"Yes. My parents died in a flu epidemic when I was five. Ellen and Abel Cooper were wonderful to me. My grandpa must have decided I was the family's only hope for preservation of his gypsy culture so he taught me how to throw knives."

"And throw them very well," Bobbi commented. "You know how skillful she is. Jaden keeps quiet about her abilities."

"For good reason." Jaden raised her hand in protest. She frowned at Roberta Petra Jones-Schmidt. "It's not something that comes up often in ordinary conversation. My love of knives came straight from the moment I first watched Grandpa put one together."

Amanda said, "An unusual talent. Is that why you bought the cutlery business, Jaden? Everyone was surprised when a woman bought the store."

As soon as the car was parked, Kyle stepped out to open the door for them. "Ladies, you are lovely. Those starlets at the academy awards could learn from you."

Jaden was glad she had worn a short black wool jacket because the new Monterey Performing Arts Center was built right on the edge of the bay about the length of a football field from the yacht harbor. She pulled her jacket tighter in the brisk, clear, December evening.

"You two look elegant in your tuxedos," Jaden returned the compliment, taking Kyle's offered arm. Bobbi took the other. A beaming Sydney escorted Amanda Perkins.

"Everyone is going to be envious of me," Kyle whispered. "I'm with two of the most beautiful ladies in the auditorium."

What a charmer, Jaden thought.

"Kyle. Jaden. Bobbi." The familiar voice belonged to Hal Lamont, the former owner of Jaden's store, who had brought his new wife, Sandy, to the opening night.

"Hal! Sandy! I didn't know that you two were back. Congratulations, again."

"Thanks, Jaden," Sandy answered. The petite woman was bucking the color trend, wearing a lavender pantsuit with an edging of crystal beads on the lapels. The suit was much more practical than the evening gowns worn by some of the women. It could be worn to a wedding or a dinner party.

Since Jaden assumed Sandy and Hal would never be married, their wedding announcement surprised her. "I hope you can run the store by yourself for a week," he told her casually one day, explaining his honeymoon plans. "I love Sandy, and I liked being married, Jaden. I've been lonesome. This will be a good move for both of us."

"Of course, Hal. That's wonderful! Take off as long as you want."

The couple were married in a small service at the Chapel-By-the-Sea at Eighth and Lincoln. Jaden, Kyle, Sydney, Bill, Bobbi, and Sandy's sister attended. Kyle and

Sydney wanted to give them a reception in the court. Hal insisted on taking them all out to The Shell Game, the best seafood restaurant in Carmel.

"You two need a night off. And this way you can critique the restaurant." Hal had told them. "But thank you very much for the offer. Sandy and I really appreciate it."

Jaden wished them congratulations and bon voyage about a week and a half ago, and had forgotten that they must be back.

As they all were walking into the theater, Sandy told them, "I am so happy that the ballet company came here. It's hard to get large, well-known groups. Most of the professional companies want a large guarantee up front. My understanding is that so many of the Kurloff company members wanted to see Monterey Bay that they came for a reduced percentage of the ticket price. About five of them had been in the Monterey area several times in the past. Frederic Melinikov loves this area. The show sold out, so the production will be doing very well financially."

The lobby, though large, was crowded with opening-nighters. It was an exciting show of the most elegant of Monterey Bay society enjoying a night that they normally would have to drive a hundred plus miles to San Francisco to experience. The huge lobby windows showed a spectacular, unusually clear view of Monterey Bay all the way to Santa Cruz at the opposite point.

"Edward, you look extremely handsome tonight," Bobbi commented. "Thank you for including us in this invitation."

"My pleasure." The general bowed slightly. His blue eyes twinkled as he looked at the group.

Jaden admired his mother, Esther, whose same light blue eyes were complimented by the soft, long, light blue dress that she wore with a blue topaz and diamond slide on her gold omega necklace. She could not be pushing eighty-seven, Jaden thought. But she is. Then she groaned to herself. Beyond Esther, heading right for them, she saw Earl "Buck" Rawlings, the mayor of Carmel, with his wife, Mrs. Mayor Constance.

Of course, naturally, they would be here. Anyone who was anybody was here.

Next to Esther Jaden saw Bill. He was holding back a little, looking glum, as he often did. Jaden suspected that he would rather be home. Incredibly handsome in that black tuxedo, though. He could easily step into a 1930's movie.

His smile, when it did come, could melt an ice sculpture. Jaden smiled back.

He was moving toward them when a petite platinum blonde in a short, short silver sequined dress walked over and threw her arms around him. She obviously knew Bill and spoke with him animatedly for a few minutes. *Old girlfriend*, Jaden knew immediately. Well, not so old. Bill smiled and hugged the blonde, then held her at arm's length, his eyes taking in her entire sensational form. Suddenly another tall man with shoulder length brown hair moved over and slipped his arm around the woman's tiny waist. The blonde introduced the two men, who shook hands. The boyfriend quickly whisked her into the crowd.

Jaden felt annoyed by her own reaction, which was jealousy mixed with relief.

"Bashful blonde," Bobbi whispered in her ear as they watched the woman being whisked into the crowd by her escort. "Just a wild guess but I believe Bill knows her."

"I believe he does, too," Kyle commented with a twinkle in his gray eyes. "But take away her face, her figure, and what do you have?"

"Plenty," Jaden muttered, embarrassed to feel her face grow warm.

"Look. Gene Miller is quite the man around town. I've never seen him wear anything but his *Welcome to Carmel* t-shirt," Bobbi said. "And he actually looks like he's had a few decent meals."

Jaden scolded herself for the obvious twinge of jealousy that she felt when the blonde hugged Bill. She had no reason to be jealous, no hold on Bill. He was an attractive man who certainly must have plenty of choices when it came to women. And when they found out he was the artist, Aram, he became the focus of the attention of complete strangers. Not quite like Frederic, who captured everyone's attention the minute he entered a room. She was glad Bill was her friend. Right now she was not ready to allow a deeper relationship to develop.

It was a struggle, though.

Bill finally made his way through the crowded lobby to join them. His eyes focused on Jaden, but he managed to say, "Ladies, how nice all of you look tonight."

An unfamiliar voice broke into their conversation, "Mayor and Mrs. Rawlings! May we have a quick word for our television audience tonight?"

The bright lights made Jaden squint.

"Of course, James." Although he was certainly no Clint Eastwood, Mayor Earl "Buck" Rawlings always turned it on for the cameras. He might not know your name, but he knew how to shake hands and how to play to the media. That appeared to be the skill necessary for today's political prizes.

She and Bobbi were two people the mayor knew very well. Jaden felt he always avoided them, though, because of their not so politically popular reputations. She knew his wife, Constance, did not want even second hand scandals to mar her husband's reputation with the media.

Constance grabbed Bill's arm. Jaden felt her own teeth grinding. The woman knew that William Aram Amirkhanian, next to the ballet company's principal dancers, was by far the most famous of the night's attendees.

"How are you enjoying this opening night, Mayor and Mrs. Rawlings?" the reporter asked, and pointed the microphone toward the mayor.

"It's an honor to have the Kurloff Ballet performing here. We feel happy to be present on this historic occasion. This is the most famous group that has ever performed in the new arts center. As you know, my wife and I are strong supporters of the arts."

The camerawoman turned toward Constance who was wearing a floor length emerald green silk designer dress with her arm entwined around Bill's so he could not escape gracefully. The camera loved Bill's dark, wavy hair and deep brown eyes. It was a politician's dream photo op.

"Is this Aram Amirkhanian?" the reporter asked, obviously impressed.

"Yes, our good friend," Constance lied smoothly through a brilliant smile.

Bill's face reddened. He was saved by the young women making their way through the crowd ringing soft bells. "Find your seats, ladies and gentlemen. Time to find your seats."

"Thank you, Mayor and Mrs. Rawlings and Mr. Amirkhanian," the reporter said gracefully, adding into the microphone. "Aram Amirkhanian is famous for his paintings of the Monterey Bay area."

"Always a pleasure, James," Buck Rawlings answered with a broad smile.

Bobbi rescued them by saying, "Oh, time to go in for the performance."

The reporter was talking to Bill alone. Bill nodded to him and turned to join them.

"What a shame." Constance frowned.

Jaden felt that Mrs. Mayor wanted to know what the reporter asked Bill. Actually, Jaden did, too.

"We don't see you often," Constance went on, "Would you...and your friends like to go out to dinner after the show?"

Jaden thought that if the mayor's wife could, she would have asked Bill alone. Notorious women like Jaden Steele and Roberta Jones-Schmidt would not help the mayor's chances to be governor.

"We should be going in." Edward saved them from having to respond no and then possibly having to explain why. Evidently no one thought to ask the mayor and his wife to attend the reception at the Seventeen-Mile-Drive home. If Constance found out, she would be livid. She considered herself Carmel's social shepherdess. *Mrs. Mayor*.

Without warning a strong hand took her arm. She felt Bill's presence next to her before she looked. "May I have the pleasure of sitting with you?" he asked, his face still pink. "I need calming. That woman...."

"She was pretty shameless tonight grabbing hold of you like that. You are her dear, dear friend," Jaden teased. "She would claim you as a godson if she could."

"Politicians!" Bill grumbled. "And their *Mrs.* politicians."

Edward's voice behind him said, "You should go to Washington, D.C. Some of those people make Constance look like an amateur. They'd sell out their friends and their grandmothers to get publicity or destroy someone. Talk about putting the country last...by God, I'm glad I'm retired!" He was tired, literally. Tired of inbred DC politics and tired of trying to explain life and death matters to politicians with hearing problems. More than once he felt tempted to say the world was coming to an end at noon just to see if one of them would react. They would probably fight to get themselves on the next spaceship out of here, at the same time trying to blame someone else for doomsday. He fortunately retired before the thought became an irreversible action.

The desire to retire to a deserted island proved tempting until he figured out how much that would cost. Besides, he knew a week by himself and he would be begging for a boat.

As an usher led them down to the captain's circle, or the best seats in the house, Jaden thought she glimpsed Gene Miller sitting to their left. She felt badly that he had not been included in their party, but he obviously had an good seat because of his work with the Monterey Dance Academy.

"These are wonderful!" Bobbi told Edward. "I must be overusing that word, but look. They're perfect. They normally must cost a fortune. "

Their seats were in the center of the auditorium about eight rows back from the orchestra pit. The group took up three-fourths of the row. Jaden and Bill were the first two in, so they went to seats eleven and twelve, right in the middle.

Kyle sat next to them, with Amanda on his left. Edward sat in the aisle seat.

"We left the Rawlings behind," Jaden whispered, surprised that she deliberately was teasing Bill.

"Good!" He sat down in his seat with his arms folded. "I hope they are nowhere near us. Buck is O.K. but that wife of his…."

"She wants Buck to be governor," Kyle whispered. "Don't you want to help?"

"Yes. If they promise they will move to Sacramento!" Bill whispered loudly.

"Let it go. Don't let one person ruin the show," Jaden ordered softly.

Bill chuckled. "Just for you, dear." He imitated Constance's inflection. His hand engulfed Jaden's and he suddenly kissed her fingers gently.

The brush of his lips was such a surprise that her whole body trembled. Goosebumps shot up her arm. She pulled her hand away. They exchanged a quick glance as the house lights dimmed. Jaden saw only the reflections of the stage lights mirrored in his dark eyes.

Applause filled the performing arts center. The tuxedoed orchestra director walked to the center of the stage and bowed to the audience applause. He walked down the steps to the orchestra pit. Everyone in the performing arts center quieted.

In the dim auditorium the inspiring strains of Tchaikovsky's overture began.

Jaden settled into her seat to enjoy being whisked into the experience. As she listened to the music that made up the overture, she realized that she had never felt this at ease with Bill before. Probably it was because of his need for post-Constance comfort, something she did not expect because he always seemed to bury his feelings in a moody gruffness.

Jaden could still feel the warm touch of his lips on her right hand. The impulsive gesture was unusual for him. Her empathy for the way the mayor's wife used him made her want to cup his left hand. Jaden resisted the temptation.

He was always controlled and, although she knew Bill was interested in her, he never pushed or insisted. Jaden suspected that his true nature was to not hold back. That's why the mayor's wife annoyed him.

The temptation to tell the woman to get lost must have been overwhelming.

Constance, don't call me Connie, could drive a lot of people to distraction.

The lithe notes of the dance of the sugar plum fairies resonated in the auditorium. "The acoustics are great," Bill whispered in her ear. Goosebumps again sprang up her arms. Luckily she was still wearing her jacket...too dark for him to see her red face.

The curtains parted to the lively opening scene of the Christmas party where Clara (one of the talented girls from the Monterey Ballet Academy) received her Nutcracker. The enchanted nutcracker was broken by Herr Drosselmeyer's nephew, Hans-Peter. Frederic danced the Nutcracker in the ballet. She did not remember meeting the dancer who played Herr Drosselmeyer. Come to think of it, Esther mentioned that he had not been feeling well the day of the tour and did not go. There were several dancers that she did recognize. Most of them, though, had been in her shop the morning that she put the display in the courtyard window. She knew that there were a few local dancers who had been hired to fill in parts. Jaden had to admire the coordination of the entire production. Several hundred people must have been involved.

The music of Tchaikovsky's masterpiece enchanted Jaden as it had millions before. The program said that it was first performed as an abridged musical score in St. Petersburg in 1892. Here it was delighting audiences a century and a half later.

Bobbi told her that the composer began the music before a tour of the United States in 1891. He finished the score after he returned to Russia.

The children from the Monterey Dance Academy were charming in the *Marche* into the party and seemed to Jaden to be close to professionals themselves. Tatiana was elegant as the Snow Queen. As she watched Clara coming to the parlor after the party to find her nutcracker, and Herr Drosselmeyer whisking her away on the magical journey, Jaden kept wondering about the theft of the

Gideon knife. For a minute, she even forgot about Bill sitting so close to her.

Days after the ballet company's visit, Jaden continued to search the shop and even the planter boxes outside in hopes of finding the missing knife. At the same time she knew one of those talented dancers stole it. She gulped. Which one?

Or, she could be wrong. If she was mistaken, where was the knife?

At the back of Jaden's mind, her sixth sense told her that a lack of money to purchase the expensive Gideon was not the reason for the theft.

The lively strains of the Trepak, the Russian Dance, filled the arts center.

Which one of those beautiful, graceful, inspiring dancers needed a knife that badly?

They were all on their feet, applauding the superb production.

"Magnificent!" Edward said. "I believe that's the best I've ever seen! Bravo!"

"I've never seen it before," Bill said, "but I can't imagine anyone not wishing Clara's dream could come true."

"You are right," Jaden said, still applauding the inspiring production.

"Jaden, I wonder what your dream is," he said.

The question startled her and tears sprang to her eyes. If only she could return to four years earlier when Brent was still alive. She almost immediately relived the nightmare day when the policewomen came to their home in Nebraska to tell her that her husband had been killed in an auto accident.

When, if ever, would that shock fade? She swallowed hard and changed the subject. "I've seen the Nutcracker in movies and on television. Edward, thank you for inviting all of us!"

Applause rose and swelled like ocean waves with each group taking bows. The final bows were first a deafening roar for Frederic Melnikov, who smiled broadly and swept his arm toward Tatiana who accepted the tribute with a graceful bow. Never to be upstaged, Frederic moved behind the ballerina and lifted her to another round of cheers and bravos.

Edward raised his voice because of the cheering, "You're welcome, but we really need to thank Igor Kurloff for the tickets. We can do that when we're backstage. We'll wait until the front rows leave or we'll be like salmon trying to swim upstream."

A girl about eight years old came onto the stage with a bouquet of red roses so large that she was hidden except for her feet. With a bow she presented the blood red flowers to Tatiana, who bowed to the audience. Cheers drowned out any chance of conversation. The dancers swept their arms toward the orchestra. The musicians and their leader took a bow. The applause began to die down and people started to slowly file out of the performing arts center.

"Come this way." Edward pointed to the stage. For a brief minute they could have been salmon trying to go upstream. Finally the crowd thinned out. They made progress toward the back stage area.

Edward presented a note from Igor Kurloff to the security guard at the short flight of stairs leading to backstage. The guard nodded and they followed the general like a short parade. Dancers and reporters crowded the area. The stage manager, Nicolas, was waiting for them. He helped begin the round of introductions.

Tatiana was first. She looked totally in control of herself and was not even perspiring. General Stennis took her graceful hand and kissed it in the finest of courtly gestures. "You were elegant and beautiful, by far the best prima ballerina performance that I have ever seen."

Tatiana flushed with pleasure and responded in her strong Russian accent, "Thank you, Edward. It is so good of you to come tonight. And here is Jaden, who owns 'A Slice of Carmel.' The cutlery store." Her blue eyes moved immediately to Bill. No mistaking that she was looking at the handsome artist with admiration. "And who is this? I am certain that we did not yet meet. Jaden, is this your husband?"

Both Jaden and Bill immediately shook their heads. Jaden felt her face flame for the second time during the evening. What was the matter with her?

Edward broke the silence by introducing Bill, "This is William Amirkhanian."

"I am so very pleased to meet you. You are Armenian?" She held out her hand.

"Congratulations on your superb performance." Imitating Edward, Bill kissed her offered hand.

The dancer smiled and withdrew her hand slowly, deliberately, and sensually, as though she were still using her expressive hands in the ballet. Her brilliant smile never left Bill's face. Jaden did not understand why the dancer's desire to impress Bill bothered her.

Edward introduced Bobbi. "I would like you to meet our good friend, Bobbi Jones."

A flicker of surprise lit the dancer's large, expressive blue eyes.

Jaden guessed that she possibly recognized Bobbi, who looked like her former self, and no longer in disguise. Two years ago her murder trial was the biggest story in the media. Anyone in the world who watched television might recognize her. She was on the cover of every tabloid. People who did not know who their senator or mayor was knew Roberta Jones-Schmidt. She was hounded so that she disguised herself and, with the help of friends like Library Director, Amanda Perkins, escaped to start a new life in Carmel.

"This is my friend, Amanda Perkins," Bobbi was saying, "and Kyle Foster and Sydney Allingham. I believe you met them at their Carmel café in Dolores Court."

"Certainly, and we had the delicious meal that day. Melon and fresh sweet strawberries," she said, holding out her hand for Kyle first.

Kyle, the tallest of all the men, kissed her hand in the most elegant manner. Sydney looked a little more awkward. He also looked a bit like Santa stuffed into a black tuxedo. Both men spoke animatedly to the ballerina for several minutes.

Jaden did not realize that one of the dancers had moved to her side until he lightly touché her shoulder.

"Jaden Steele. How did you like the performance?" The only name that came to her mind was Fred Astaire. But she knew that the voice with a charming, precise accent belonged to Frederic Melnikov.

"It was wonderful," she answered sincerely, wondering how she could have missed the gaudy red hair even in a crowd.

"I danced because I knew you were in the audience."

"Now, Frederic...." That was laying it on a bit thick. She sensed how easy it was for Frederic to snare women. Actually they probably wanted to be snared. His personality was magnetic on and off stage. In self-defense she took Bill's arm.

She noticed Tatiana excuse herself to no doubt go to the dressing room to change.

"Frederic, I'd like you to meet a good friend, Bill Amirkhanian."

Bill was about a head taller than Frederic. He held out his free right hand to the dancer who looked a bit disappointed.

"So very glad to meet you, Bill. You are Jaden's friend?" Emphasis on Jaden.

A quick smile came to Bill's lips and he said in a teasing manner, "I am tonight."

Jaden gave him a grateful smile, which he returned quickly.

Frederic turned to Bobbi, who looked exceptionally glamorous. The brown velvet was perfect for her. Jaden could not help thinking back to when she first met Bobbi. She was wearing a too large black suit that looked like she was trying out for a witch's part. Bobbi's lack of taste in clothes was so bad that Jaden had sensed something wrong.

"This is my friend, Roberta Jones."

This time Frederic took her hand and kissed it with a flourish. No mistaking that he recognized her when he asked, "Have we met before?"

Bobbi glanced at Jaden, and saw that her friend had a slight twinge of pink coloring her high cheekbones.

"You may have seen my picture in a newspaper or on television, Frederic."

"You are an actress?" Frederic was obviously trying to connect the dots.

The stage manager walked over with the dancer who had played Herr Drosselmeyer. "Ladies and gentlemen, please allow me to introduce Boris ."

"We are delighted," Kyle answered for them, "Your performance was inspired."

The dancer, about four inches taller than Frederic with brown hair slicked down, smiled broadly. "Thank you," he said. "So nice to meet you." Boris, obviously not as proficient with English as Tatiana or Frederic, spoke each word slowly.

Frederic said something in Russian to the stage manager, Nicolas. Then to the visitors he said, "I asked if I could introduce you since I now know all of your names, your first names certainly."

"Boris, this is Jaden...." A sudden scream echoed in the backstage area. Everyone in the crowd stopped talking.

They froze for a moment as though they were playing a children's game of statues. Bill and then Jaden reacted first, running toward the sound of the scream.

Boris shouted, "Tatiana!"

"She's in the dressing room," someone said. "Help her!"

The frantic screams continued to echo in the backstage area.

Following Boris, the crowd of dancers, backstage personnel, and visitors all rushed toward the chilling screams.

The dressing room door was closed.

"Don't wait!!" Frederic yelled.

He almost ripped open the door. Jaden could not quite see into the room because several of the men rushed in. After a few seconds some of the people who had rushed to the door drew back, gasping. Jaden could see in to what looked like splashes of red paint on the floor. Except she knew it was not paint. The smell plunged into her nostrils. She felt woozy but shook off the wave of nausea. Thinking rapidly, she forced her eyes to scan as much of the floor as possible looking for the murder weapon.

Bill stepped forward. "Call 911!" he cried over Tatiana's screams.

Amanda pulled her cell phone from her purse and, with shaking fingers, dialed.

"Ask for detectives from the Monterey station, too, and we'll need a forensic team." Bill ordered. He stepped toward the body slumped on the floor and felt for a pulse in the neck. He shook his head.

Jaden's body shook with a silent scream.

Bobbi took one look into the room and groaned. She whirled and rushed right into Edward's arms, gasping, "Not again!"

Edward held her tightly for a few seconds until Amanda came over to them.

"Bobbi, come with me. You have to get away from here! Let's go into the auditorium and sit down. There's a water cooler over here. I'll get some water."

Bobbi did not argue.

Jaden knew that it must have reminded Bobbi of her husband's death. Knives frightened the librarian. She rarely came into the shop. After a minute or two she had to leave. To most it did not seem rational. Jaden understood perfectly. She still trembled when she remembered finding Sergio's body in the parking garage below the court.

Several of the dancers rushed to Tatiana and hugged her. They almost dragged her out of the room. Her shrieks finally stopped and she began to sob in huge gulps.

Bill ordered, "Don't anyone touch anything, please. Leave the room until the police arrive. He is dead. Nothing can be done for him."

"Who is dead?" The question echoed from several people in the crowd.

"Igor," Edward Stennis told the crowd, his voice wavering, "Igor Kurloff."

Some of the company were sobbing. Others muttered.

Boris grumbled, "America. So violent."

Igor's brother shouted and ran up to Bill, "Igor? Igor? Who would do this?"

Bill tried to push him back, but he was a strong man. "Sir. Please. Ladies and gentlemen. I am very sorry. Please stay out of the room It's a crime scene. He is dead."

More cries filled the crowded hall.

"Edward, would you stay by the door?" Bill asked. Edward nodded. "Please. I am a police officer. Everyone must stay here." He knew that most of the audience had already left. "No one leaves. I know it's late and you are all tired. You must stay here! The best thing to do is go into the auditorium and wait. I'm sorry."

"May I see him, please?" Nicolas begged. "Sir, my brother!"

Bill and Edward looked at each other. Edward nodded.

"I didn't close the door all the way because of prints. Obviously any fingerprints that may have been on the knob have been ruined," Bill said. "I'll take you in. Be careful. Very sorry. I'm in deep sympathy with how you feel but you may not disturb anything. Do you understand, Mr. Kurloff?"

His craggy features hardening, the man nodded. Bill pushed the top of the door with his hand covered by a handkerchief. They stepped in.

Nicolas moaned, "Oh, no. Oh. No!"

The blood in the room glistened in the bright light from the overhead fixtures.

"Who did this?" Nicolas' roar echoed in the room and in the whole backstage area.

It rumbled in Jaden's head.

Bill held Igor's brother's shaking shoulders. "So sorry."

"Who did this? I will kill him!" A bear-like roar rumbled from deep inside the man's chest. "Find him for me!"

"Let's go outside in the hall," Bill's voice sounded commanding and steady.

"No! No! Not my brother!" The choked words echoed like another roar in the small room. He began alternating between muttering and shouting in Russian.

Bill turned the man around and pushed him step by step from the room. Jaden thought he would resist. Nicolas emerged in the hall with eyes glazed.

"Please, everyone," Bill ordered. "Would you all take seats?"

Once in the auditorium, Bill began to confer with the Monterey police officers. Other officers swarmed in, most heading backstage, some standing at the exits.

The rapid pulsing in Jaden's throat was

dying down so slowly that she had not been able to say much except single words since they found the body. She desperately wanted to search the floor of the room for what she guessed must be the missing knife from her store. *It must be there,* she imagined, her mind whirling. *If only she had not put the knives in the window that day!*

Someone deliberately stole the knife from her store display. They had planned the murder of Igor.

Maybe my imagination is jumping too fast. Knives were easy to find anywhere. Jaden knew one thing that haunted her. *My first instincts usually were correct.*

"Bill," one of the Monterey officers was saying, "from your description it was chaos backstage after the show. We will interview everyone who hasn't left."

"Most of the audience is gone. You will interview the cast and orchestra. Take as many notes as possible. Maybe some stories will show up as inconsistent."

"Bill, we're going to be the rest of the week just entering these interviews into the computer," the officer said.

The concessionaires brought hot coffee and cookies into the auditorium and set them in front of the orchestra pit on a newly arrived card table.

"The concession people should stay, shouldn't they, sergeant?" one of the officers asked the man to whom Bill had been speaking.

The sergeant nodded yes.

Buck Rawlings was complaining to one of the officers, "Look here, my man. I am the mayor of Carmel. You can trust my wife and me to come to the Monterey station tomorrow. We don't know anything about this. My wife is very tired."

"Mr. Mayor," the officer was obviously trying to keep his voice level, "You will have to speak to the lieutenant. When he is free, I'll take you over. I'm sorry, sir."

Buck Rawlings huffed, grumbled, and went to report his conversation to his wife, who loudly demanded, "Did you tell him who you are?"

Buck Rawlings sank into a seat, closed his eyes, and nodded.

Constance was still jabbering angrily at him as Jaden walked away. Buck slumped in his seat. She noticed Gene standing near the coffee table. "Gene! Come join us."

"Jaden, can you tell me what happened? I'm exhausted and would love to go home. I have an appointment tomorrow for a buyer for one of Bill's paintings. Someone's been knifed? After such a beautiful performance."

As she explained what had happened Gene turned paler and paler. She led him over to where the members of their party were sitting.

The first person to be interviewed was the dancer who played several parts in the production, Maria Essipov, who had looked so elegant on stage. Now her face was pale as snow. She continually rubbed her hands together as though they were freezing. Because she was uncomfortable with English, Edward was translating, which made the interview take twice as long.

"My mother also can translate for the non-English speakers, Lieutenant Cooper," Edward told the interviewing officers. He showed them one card that must have been very impressive credentials.

Esther had been circulating through the crowd at the auditorium. As a little old woman, she looked inconspicuous and distracted. Jaden knew that Esther would not miss a thing. Carmel's own version of Miss Marple was jotting notes in that observant brain. She had a better memory than people half her age. "Almost photographic when I was young. Scored the highest of anyone ever on the observation test. One officer thought I had cheated until I turned around and told him everything he was wearing and that he had cut himself shaving," she told

Jaden one day. "Old age has stolen a lot of it from me."

"That's good that someone speaks Russian!" the lieutenant answered. "Let's find out how many need a translator. I don't want to use the English speaking members of the company because they are all suspects. Actually, you are, too." He grinned quickly and just as quickly returned a serious, official mask to his face.

Maria's face was growing whiter until it reminded Jaden of a fine porcelain cup. She decided to pour her a cup of coffee. At the risk of interrupting the interview, she offered it to the dancer who accepted with sweating hands. Tears brimmed in her hazel eyes. She nodded a thank you.

Sandy, Hal, Gene, and Sydney were sitting together in the next row, leaning toward Kyle who was saying, "I can't believe we went from elation about the show to this. Who could have wanted to destroy the company? It's impossible to believe."

Sandy said, "Maybe someone was trying to rob him. But how did they get in?"

Jaden felt certain the motive was not a robbery. He must have been slashed several times. Her senses screamed that the physical evidence indicated deep hatred. And how could anyone do that and not be noticed when he or she left?

With shaking hands she poured herself a cup of coffee and stared into the steaming, dark liquid. She tried to go over everything that happened after the last curtain call. Officer Martinez asked Maria, "Had you seen Igor Kurloff at all?" Yes and no. Maria was positive that he had appeared backstage several times after the intermission. Since he was a fixture backstage, company members did not notice him because of the pre-performance turmoil, dressing, make-up, helping the mothers with the children, all of which provided a good reason why he was not noticed. Later he may have been around, but she actually did not see him. He could not have been dead in the dressing room when Tatiana was dressing to perform. Or, he may have been there. That made the famous ballerina the chief suspect. She kept thinking about Tatiana's interest in the window display the day Edward brought the company members into her store.

When was he killed? Jaden knew that the medical examiners, a photographer, and crime scene technicians were in the murder room now. Like Maria, she felt icy cold.

Bobbi came up to her looking almost as pale as Maria. "How are you doing?"

"Not well. I keep thinking about Igor bleeding to death. He might have been in the room for precious minutes losing blood."

"I...I was so shocked seeing all that blood. He was not there for hours, Jaden. It was Tatiana's dressing room. She was there several times during the Nutcracker. Someone attacked him after her last costume change. There was prolonged applause."

"You're right, of course, Bobbi. The killer knew everyone would be distracted." That meant someone knew the backstage routine. She lowered her voice, "Did I tell you about the knife that was stolen from the store when the company was there?"

Bobbi's almond shaped eyes slanted even more when she was in deep thought. "Do you believe that was the weapon?"

"I hope I'm wrong but the theft keeps nagging at me. Why would a company dancer risk being arrested for theft? If I'm right, that means the murder was planned."

"Let's wait. I'm sure they will find the weapon. Two detectives plus a forensic team are searching the dressing rooms and all of the backstage area now."

"If only I had not done the display that morning! I'm sure the murder weapon was the stolen knife. It was sharp enough. "

"Jaden, how can you feel guilty? Besides, you're guessing. If someone were that set on murder they would have stolen a weapon some other way. You know almost any object can be a murder weapon in the wrong person's hand." Bobbi hugged her.

Jaden groaned and shook her head. "Do you really feel all right? Bobbi, the blinding red, the sweet smell of blood. It was like finding Sergio in the garage."

"Well, I don't feel like I'm going to throw up any more. I just had a sandwich for dinner because we were going to that reception in Pebble Beach. Now, in spite of what's happened, I'm starving."

Jaden realized that she was hungry, too. Cookies were no help. Bobbi loved a good meal. Unlike Jaden, who had to watch herself, the librarian never seemed to put on any weight.

Her head was pounding by five a.m, the time the fifty or so company members and auditorium employees were finally finished being interviewed by Bill and the Monterey lieutenant. The lucky ones who left at the end of the show escaped the all night questioning ordeal.

"Ladies and gentlemen," Lt. Cooper finally told the crowd, "we finished our preliminary questions and you are free to go." A collective groan of relief echoed in the theater. "We may contact some of you again. Don't worry if that happens. We probably want clarification of something in our notes."

Even in the cold, dripping mist every seagull on Monterey Bay knew it was morning. Daylight meant the eternal search of the beach and the coastal city for food.

They were circling high over the parking lot, sounding so much like barking dogs. Their barking was joined by the deeper chorus of sea lions on the shoreline rocks.

The wet, cold December morning made Jaden pull her jacket tightly around her until they slipped into the back seat of the Lincoln. Bill stayed with the Monterey Police, but pale-faced Gene walked out with them. He was wearing a long gray wool topcoat perfect for this morning. "I've got to go back and get some sleep. I have an appointment at one with a buyer who is interested in the Aram that I have on display in the gallery window."

Jaden swallowed hard. She knew how she would miss that beautiful work of art. It would be like losing a friend.

With the possibility of that kind of a sale, she knew Gene Miller would drag himself to his gallery.

"Selling that ought to make Bill happy, in spite of the murder," Edward commented. "It would be a high and a low point in twenty-four hours, wouldn't it? This is a nightmare. I'm desperate to wake up."

"I can cook breakfast for us," Sydney offered as they stood outside the car.

"You deserve a break," Edward said. "You cook every day. I think there's a twenty-four hour restaurant on Lighthouse Avenue, a block up from the aquarium. Breakfast is my treat."

Although Kyle made a face to show what he thought of twenty-four hour restaurants, he walked over to Hal and Sandy and told them.

"They're going to meet us in Pacific Grove," he told the car's occupants.

Then he walked back and opened his car's trunk. He returned to the driver's side with a blanket. "Ladies."

Jaden snuggled under the soft fleece.

The forty degree morning was normal for the coast this time of year. Summers would be warm at seventy degrees. Most of the rest of the country, even the central valley of California, would love the mild summer. Why was she thinking about the weather of all things? It was December.

This could not be normal thinking. She was exhausted, hungry, and, at the same time, sick to her stomach every time she thought of seeing the murdered man.

The night had not been normal. Waiting to be questioned by the police and seeing the murdered man over and over in her mind was unbearable. The continual vision of the murdered Igor circled in her thoughts like a carousel. With icy hands Jaden gratefully unfolded the blanket so it covered Amanda, Bobbi, and herself. By the time they left the parking lot, Jaden's exhausted eyes closed to a dark, quiet world.

Her mind swirled into a mist. She was in the driver's seat of a car. Not driving. The car sped wildly forward out of her control. She grabbed the wheel. Nothing happened. She could not steer. The car flew over the edge of a cliff, diving into space.

Bobbi gently woke her by shaking her shoulder. Jaden's eyes opened slowly and she said, "What a horrible dream." She saw that they were in a parking lot off Lighthouse Avenue. "Oh, no! It wasn't a nightmare. Someone killed Igor Kurloff!"

Sydney was opening the door for her. "Careful, Jaden. I know you were asleep."

With a deep sigh she stepped into the foggy Pacific coast morning.

"No. It wasn't," Bobbi commented.

Once inside the warm, almost empty restaurant, they were shown to a booth big enough for the nine of them to be cozy. The staff added a table for four in front of the booth's table. Sandy and Hal joined them Without Bill they made an unlucky party of thirteen. And they did not need any more bad luck.

Of course the bad luck had already happened. By this time she expected to be in bed under her cozy down comforter. Could things get any worse? And she hated to admit it to herself, but she missed having Bill with them. What he must be going through with all of the statements and reports. The forensic team would certainly be in the middle or finishing with their investigation of the murder scene.

"I'm going to eat the menu," Bobbi said. "I'm ashamed after all that's happened."

How can she do that? Jaden wondered. Her own stomach felt queasy.

The waitress distributed the plastic encased menus. The shiny plastic reflected in the overhead lights, making Jaden's eyes hurt as she tried to read.

"Who would like coffee?" The waitress, Minnie, asked.

Was that really her name? Jaden dug her reading glasses out of her evening bag.

Eight of them signaled yes. Kyle pursed his lips, "As long as it's not in one of those dreadful Styrofoam cups."

Minnie gave him a quick glance and an "I've heard it all before" nod.

"Could I have tea, please?" Sandy asked.

"Certainly," Minnie said. A busboy came over to fill the cups of the caffeine-addicted. "I wish we could have coffee from the Mad Hatters," Edward said after one sip.

"We do have the best," Kyle admitted smugly. "Like Edison, it took us years of experiments to find success with *the* blend."

"Now the doctor has asked me to cut down to one cup of coffee a day." Sydney, who barely fit into the booth, complained, "Easy for him to prescribe. I love coffee."

"It's for your own good," Kyle responded. "Your blood pressure…."

Sydney answered with a frown. "Let's not talk about our ailments."

"We should eat and get back to rest," Kyle told them. "At least we're closed today. Closed Sunday and Monday during these three months."

Post-holiday from the end of December through February were usually quieter in Carmel, but the tourist trade was unpredictable. The holidays, Lincoln and Washington's birthdays, now president's day, the AT&T Golf Tournament brought in good business. And in August the Concours d'Elegance with the beautifully restored cars on display always filled the sidewalks with tourists. Between Jaden and Hal they tried to keep the shop open six days a week. Monday was their closed day until March. She sighed. Here she was thinking about business after that horrible murder.

The vision of Igor's body covered in blood stabbed into her mind. She almost dropped her coffee cup. Coffee splashed into the saucer and on the table.

"Oh, I'm sorry!" She grabbed her napkin to wipe up the coffee.

Bobbi, sitting next to her, used her napkin, too. "Never mind, Jaden. We're all shaky right now. Dolores Court is going to be quiet with the shops closed."

The waitress slipped Edward's omelet in front of him and noticed the spilled coffee. "You had the biscuits and gravy." She put that in front of Sydney with an extra pitcher of gravy. "I'll send the busboy over with a fresh cup of coffee for you."

"Thank you." Jaden could not help feeling sheepish, like a child who spilled her milk. The moist, warm smell of her scrambled eggs and toast banished all of her other thoughts. She could barely hold off until everyone received his breakfast.

"In my wildest imagination," Kyle dug into his hash browns, "I never would have guessed there would be a murder and we would stay up all night to answer police questions instead of partying on Seventeen Mile Drive. Did I know Igor? *Met him once on their visit twelve years earlier to perform in Monterey.* What did I think of him? I really didn't think much beyond that he was the founder and manager of the famous ballet company."

"I don't believe people liked him," Esther began. She seemed to be the only one of them who was not tired. Maybe when you get to be eighty plus you want to take advantage of the short time left to you and you don't sleep as much.

Hal actually laughed. "No, Esther, someone did not like him."

Esther went on, "You know how people behave when someone they like dies? "This was different. As I was circulating, waiting my turn to be questioned, I certainly did not get the impression that many people would miss Igor."

Edward stared at his mother without comment. He knew how well she observed. Jaden already guessed something like that from what she noticed in the store. And Tatiana was crying more because of the shock of discovering the killing than from losing her husband. Or, she may have been performing. Maybe she did slash him. Nothing unique about killings in families. And Tatiana had been so interested in her store's knife display.

She suddenly felt that Bobbi might be acting, too. The sight of a person killed like that must have reminded her of her abusive, dead husband lying on the kitchen floor after their struggle for the knife. Although she had a restraining order, he broke into the house. In Bobbi's desperate fight to get away from the drunken man, he slipped and fell on the blade.

To add to Bobbi's shock, the District Attorney tried her for murder. Bobbi was the media sensation for months. The tabloids missed not a minute of her life. *GLAMOUROUS LIBRARIAN IN LOVE TRYST* was one Jaden remembered. *Men whom Bobbi barely knew wrote stories like I DATED ROBERTA. INTIMATE BEDROOM SECRETS* was another. *INNOCENT OR COLD-BLOODED KILLER?* The tabloids made it sound like Bobbi slept with everyone she met. Pure fiction whipped up by hack writers paid for their warped creativity. What a nightmare for her.

Jaden turned to her friend and asked, "How are you doing, Bobbi?"

The woman's golden flecked eyes blinked. "All right. When I saw the body, I felt sick to my stomach. Every memory of my husband's death flooded back. I thought those were buried, but they're not. Are they always going to be there? Why can't I forget? It could have been yesterday."

Edward broke in, "Bobbi, be patient. The nightmare will fade in time."

"I don't think I am going to live that long," she responded bitterly, jabbing her fork at a sausage.

Edward knew too much about post-traumatic stress. Some memories do stay vivid forever.

"Does everyone else feel the same way I do?" Jaden asked. "His wife, Tatiana, will be the main suspect." Tatiana was so interested in the knives.

They all nodded except for Edward and Esther.

Esther said, "Right now there are about forty suspects. But love and money are constant reasons for murder. Remember Vincent Howard? He killed for both."

"I'm never going to forget Vincent or Marian Panetti," Jaden said quietly. The subject of the murders brought her to full wakefulness. At the same time she knew the frightening memories would keep her wide awake for the rest of the day.

"I hope Marian stays in that institution up north." Amanda commented, opening a teaspoon-sized packet of what she suspected was colored sugar jelly. "It's too easy for her to get out of a place like that."

Staring at the small scars on her forearms, Jaden remembered the crazed, wild-eyed woman. Sometimes she would have a nightmare of returning to that scene in the shop when Marian fired the gun. Because of her insanity, the woman never stood trial for Vincent's murder. Shouldn't there be a plea of guilty but insane? Justice was blind.

"I need to find some answers," Jaden mumbled, almost to herself.

"We're in the same boat," Bobbi answered. "Where could we begin? Unless the police find the murder weapon, we will never know if what you suspect is right."

"What do you suspect, Jaden?" Sydney poured more gravy on his biscuits. "If you can catch the waitress's attention, I'd like another biscuit."

Kyle glared at him and almost hissed, "You do not need another biscuit."

"But it's not going to come out even." He looked around the table, appealing for support that did not come. "He never lets me have this at home."

"It's for your own good." Kyle protested. "Then you wonder why you have the weight and the cholesterol problems!"

The group at the table all laughed. Jaden barely controlled her laugh at Sydney. His face looked like a little boy whose candy was stolen.

Sydney glanced up, his face red. He looked down at his almost empty plate and said with a sigh. "Look at Bobbi eating that so-called jelly. It's probably nothing but colored sugar. Life is not fair."

"No, it's not," tall, thin Kyle agreed.

"It was my favorite breakfast as a kid," Sydney told them. "My mom saved all the grease from the day before and made gravy for the leftover biscuits. It was a way to feed five boys. My dad was a farmworker in the Central Valley. He probably never made more than $300 a month in his whole life. The farmer gave him a house and a steady job so we never had to move. He and his wife had no children and were really nice to us. Of all the boys I was his wife's favorite. We had plenty of freedom to play. Never knew we were poor."

"Nobody thought about diets then," Amanda commented. "Now we have three shelves of diet books and people want more. The Mad Hatter's has a healthy menu."

"Your food is great," Bobbi said.

Kyle added, "Thanks, ladies."

Minnie came over with the check, which Edward quickly grabbed. "You liked your biscuits and gravy," she told Sydney with a smile. "That milk gravy's made right here. Not out of a can like some places."

Sydney nodded. "Very good."

Jaden thought that the chef felt he could make a superior gravy but was too polite to say so. He still managed to clean his plate sans biscuit so that it hardly needed rinsing.

Kyle was right, of course. There was no way he would change Sydney. She always thought that cooks cooked because they loved food. It was a stereotype that Sydney fit perfectly.

"I am exhausted," Sandy admitted. "First the flight home. Then this."

Edward signed the bill and they all filed back to the cars.

Jaden had barely two hours sleep before she had to open the shop. Bill stopped by about 10:30 a.m., his pale face resembling the color of Maria Essipov's during her early morning questioning.

Staring at him, Jaden swallowed hard, resisting the temptation to grab his arm and lead him upstairs. "You should be in bed."

"In about two minutes, Jaden. I thought you would want to know that we never found the murder weapon. Everyone was searched. I realized that you believe the weapon used was the Gideon knife stolen from your shop."

"I do. It's too much of a coincidence."

"I've told the coroner and she may want to borrow one to compare slash marks."

"I understand. Thank you." Jaden repeated, "Now go upstairs and get some sleep." In a gesture that was uncharacteristic for her, she touched his hand. His fingers were long and delicate, an artist's fingers. He had an athlete's body, though, strong and well-trained.

He grinned weakly. "Yes, ma'am. Sleep sounds like heaven. But I know your mind, Jaden. You are tenacious, like a bulldog."

"Isn't that romantic," slipped out before she could stop herself.

She knew he would not have said bulldog if he had not been so tired. Jaden had to smile at how accurate he was about her stubborn desire to find out all the answers. There were a lot of people smarter than she was, but not many who kept driving forward until they hit their target.

"Maybe I will see you tonight or tomorrow morning." His eyes did not have the sparkle that they normally did when he was asking her for a date. They were red-rimmed set in dark sockets.

"Of course you will." She watched him leave the shop and slowly climb the open concrete steps to the second floor apartments.

Jaden often wondered if she should have left her comfortable, protected university teaching position to come to Carmel. *I fell in love with the wild, restless ocean before I imagined myself in love with a womanizing, married man.* A wise woman would never have fallen for a creep like Sergio. It was the biggest mistake of her life and she vowed to never repeat suspending her common sense.

She stared at the empty patio tables. Everyone else had gone to bed and maybe she should have, too. If she had stayed in Nebraska, though, she never would have met Kyle or Sydney, Bill, Bobbi, fascinating Esther and her son, Edward, or the attorney, McKenzie Anderson, who reminded Jaden so much of her husband, Brent.

Hal, the former owner of the business, interrupted her thoughts by walking into the shop. He also owned the entire court, and, she guessed, more property in Carmel.

"Jaden, I thought you might need a break for a while."

"You weren't supposed to come into the shop until tomorrow."

"After last night, there was no way I could rest. I tried. Finally gave up. Let me at least give you a break. You are exhausted."

"I slept for a couple of hours with never-ending nightmares until I got up myself. Bill just came by. He looked barely able to move. He's upstairs in bed, I hope. The whole investigation team was up all night and now it's almost noon."

"I know Bill often stays up late painting. Up all night and most of the morning is too much even for a gifted artist. Evil does get to him. Killing Igor Kurloff was a crime of pure hate." Hal paused and took in a breath. "You like Bill, don't you?"

Jaden stared at Hal's clear blue eyes. Although he obviously wanted an answer, she did not speak.

"I know it's none of my business." Hal went on, "Don't be afraid because of that worthless Sergio, Jaden. God knows how many poor relationships I had after my wife died. I made a lot of mistakes, but finally found Sandy. I do love her."

"You are good together, Hal."

"Thank you, Jaden," he said with a grin. "What I'm trying to say is don't wait too long. Don't be afraid to take chances."

When she did not respond he continued, "Some people want their house perfectly clean before they will go outside. Often that means that they never leave the house."

When Jaden did not speak, Hal decided that those beautiful violet eyes were telling him, *You're right. It is none of your business. Enough advice.*

She decided to take a quick walk to avoid any further discussion. "Thanks, Hal. Fresh air will clear my mind. Maybe I'll walk over to the library and say hi to Bobbi or just sit in the sun at the park."

She left for the short walk to Lincoln Street. While the tourists jostled her, she admitted to herself that she was afraid of any new relationship.

How could Hal be so right? She did not want to leave her safe little apartment world. Jaden wove her way through tourists who were staring into shop windows and reading restaurant menus.

Jaden must have looked like a total native because a man with a camera dangling from a neck strap caught her eye. "Miss, could you tell me where we can find the First Murphy House?"

His smile banished her confused thoughts. They were standing almost diagonally across from First Murphy Park. "Right over there. It's hidden by the trees and bushes."

The U shape of the three benches at the corner backed by burgundy azaleas, successfully hid the house and the other facilities in the park. A Japanese tourist was taking a picture of his wife sitting on the first bench next to the bronze statue of the Valentine couple, probably the most photographed spot in the city. Jaden stared at the corner, at the middle bench that faced Sixth Street. Sitting on the bench set back from the street were Frederic and Gene. Jaden blinked to make certain that she was seeing correctly. There was no mistaking that unusual color of dark red hair. Even sitting on the bench across the street, Frederic's athletic body was quickly recognizable. Whatever the conversation was it was so intense that the men were not noticing anything happening around them. A cry of surprise died on Jaden's dry lips.

"Jaden," said a soft, familiar voice from behind her. She whirled to see Esther.

"What are you staring at, Jaden?"

"Esther," Jaden actually whispered for no other reason than being unable to conceal her surprise. "Look at the middle bench and tell me who you see. Maybe I'm exhausted and imagining things."

Esther's blue eyes darted quickly to the opposite corner. Her normally passive-under-most-circumstance face showed complete surprise. Her lips parted and she whispered, "Let's go into the library. Quickly, Jaden."

They turned left on Lincoln and walked rapidly down to the brick path that led through the library garden, and turned left again to walk up the brick steps to the main entry door.

"Come downstairs with me, Jaden. I'll put my purse in the workroom." Esther and Sydney were both library volunteers.

Once inside the basement workroom, they saw Bobbi at her computer. She smiled when she saw them and asked, "Are you as exhausted as I am? You should be in bed."

"Can you take a break?" Jaden asked.

Bobbi's eyes glinted with curiosity. "Of course." She stood up. "Would you like some tea? Let's go into the kitchen."

They followed Bobbi into the tiny kitchen off of the workroom. She filled a warming pot with water and plugged it in. "What's up?"

"You won't believe who is in the park across the way," Jaden told her.

"Frederic," Esther commented.

"You mean the dancer, Frederic Melnikov?" Bobbi's golden-hazel eyes glowed as she pulled out a basket filled with several different tea bags. "You're right. I'm more than surprised."

The obliging pot steamed in seconds as the librarian pulled three mugs from the cupboard and poured steaming water into each one.

"Frederic was talking to Gene, the art gallery owner." Jaden chose an English breakfast tea from the basket.

"His appearance here today is extremely odd, I have to say. More than extreme, if that is possible." Esther stirred her tea slowly, all the time peering into the steaming brew as if she saw something there. Jaden knew her mind was whirling.

"Frederic and Gene. Certainly an unlikely combination. Before work I was looking up the formation of the Kurloff Ballet Company. Right now I'm getting publicity stuff. Frederic is one of the artistic directors. Now he will certainly be my first focus as far as my computer investigations will go. And what do you really know about Gene Miller?"

"Nothing. I can't see him ever causing problems for anyone, though. He's not the type. Totally serious about his business." Jaden sipped her tea. "That's delicious."

"Frederic and Gene know each other," Esther told them. "Never go by personality alone. Some criminals can be charming."

"But Frederic Melnikov is one of the world's most famous dancers."

"Famous people can be criminals, too, Jaden. You would be surprised at the well-known crooks I have met in my life."

In her life as a spy, Jaden thought.

Esther's instincts were sharp. She focused the same way Jaden focused when she was knife throwing. Jaden certainly realized that the two men had not been talking as though they were strangers. They knew each other. "Why didn't Frederic just go to the gallery?"

"Good question." Jaden stirred her tea. "Because there is some kind of a secret."

Bobbi and Esther possessed Jaden's same burning curiosity. Bill could call them bulldogs as much as he wanted. Still, she realized that trait was the cause of trouble.

Esther stood up. "So far there are a lot more suspects than Frederic." She washed and dried her coffee mug. "But during an investigation no one can be ruled out, especially after we saw them together. I'm going to start shelving books. You will keep me informed, my darling sleuths?"

"My pleasure," Bobbi said. "Yes, I will keep you informed, Esther. We'll gather some notes and probably have a meeting in the next couple of days to compare the information to see if we notice more out of the ordinary behaviors."

Since little escaped Esther's clear blue eyes she might spot something that neither of them had noticed.

She washed and dried her mug and put it in the cupboard. "I'd better go back, too,

Bobbi. You must know that I came down to find out about your internet investigation. Have you found anything interesting or out of place?"

"Nothing really. I did a half hour's research before work. It's ballet company publicity stuff. I'll bring you the printouts. Now Frederic will be the first person for me to investigate."

"Bobbi, there are so many people involved in the company that it's going to be like sorting out a jigsaw puzzle. I hate those things. I'm too impatient to sit there for hours studying each piece. There's always one missing that holds up putting the rest of the puzzle together. Or, you've used everything and still have a missing piece."

"Yes, I know. If you look at the whole pile of crooked cardboard pieces it usually seems overwhelming. Piece by piece is the way to do one, Jaden. And sometimes you're just looking at the piece upside down or sideways. Piece by piece."

A quick smile crossed Jaden's lips.

"That's the only way to do anything."

Jaden did not take the normal way out of the library basement door, which was to go left up Ocean Street to the corner and turn left on Dolores. This time she retraced her steps deliberately to go back to the corner of Sixth and Lincoln Streets. All three of the benches across the street, except for the eternal bronze couple, were empty. Puzzled, she walked past the Little Swiss Café, a gallery, a shop that specialized in Italian ceramics, and two more art galleries.

She knew how much the leases of these stores were. *How do they all pay them?* Hal gave her a big discount on her lease for the first two years that was probably the difference between staying in business and closing the doors. She crossed the corner at Dolores and Sixth to walk the block back into the court. Only one of the outdoor tables was occupied.

The lighted Christmas tree in the street facing window of her store was the first thing that caught her eye. Hal must have turned it on. She was too foggy to remember that this morning. This afternoon a combination of tourists and locals sat at the outdoor tables in the court. Mrs. Van Dussen was enjoying tea with her two poodles, Samantha and Greyling. She was handing a bite of a scone to the cream-colored, rotund, Samantha.

"Good afternoon, Mrs. Van Dussen." *Carmelites love their dogs. This one might die of love.* She noticed that Arizona was surveying the court from her favorite high, sphinx-like perch at the top of the stairs. Because of the dogs, her fluffy white tail was whipping back and forth in an imitation of a furry snake. Like her human counterpart, Esther, the cat's half closed eyes missed nothing. If one of the dogs ventured up the steps, Jaden wondered if the huge cat would retreat or attack.

"Hello, Jaden. How are you? Samantha took the last dog biscuit from Gene's container by the gallery door. Greyling needs a treat, too, don't you, precious?"

Waddling Greyling, fatter than Samantha, always looked pregnant. She needed more walks. Kindness could be life-threatening for the overweight pooches.

Jaden glanced over to see the California gallery closed. Gene was always open. There was too much competition for him to close it unless he was sick. He could, like the rest of them, have been exhausted. Had he gone home to sleep? Or somewhere with Frederic? Her mind reeled with possibilities, all of them suspicious. Then she remembered. He had a possible buyer for Bill's seascape. He usually discussed sale possibilities with Bill. Why chat with Frederic in the park and not the gallery?

"I'm sure Gene and Frederic know each other. How is that possible?"

The bell tied to the inside of the front door rang as she thoughtfully entered.

Hal looked up. "Hi, Jaden. Good sales while you were gone."

"That's great, Hal. It looks quiet around here." *That will help me pay you*. She was in debt to Hal for the next five years for the cutlery business, and he still owned all of the court property. Then she would only have the lease to pay, plus the myriad taxes and fees dreamed up by every federal, state, and city agency in existence.

"A man stopped in to see you. He left his card with a message on the back. It's on your desk."

"Salesman?"

"No. One of the famous dancers from the Nutcracker. In fact, I believe he danced the part of the Nutcracker. Dyed red hair. Frederic. You must have made an impression on him."

Jaden took in a deep breath. "Frederic?" *He came from the park to here. Where was Gene?* Logically, they should have walked over here together. She remembered that Gene said something about appointments. Glancing through the window at the closed gallery made her gulp. The window was empty. Had Gene sold the Carmel beach scene? With the absence of the painting, she felt as though she had lost a good friend.

That's it! He sold it, maybe to Frederic, and could afford to close for a few days. There could not be many other explanations.

Hal went on, "Melnikov was really disappointed that you weren't here. Something tells me that you have a fan."

Normally, she might be delighted that she had missed Frederic, who was obviously used to charming women. And in turn, there was no lack of women who would be

delighted with his attention. He certainly
had been trying to charm her, too, before the
murder. She should be flattered. Instead, her
curiosity was running wild.

Curiosity still killed cats.

She felt she needed to talk to Bill about
Frederic and Gene.

"I am not going to wake him." Jaden
was looking at Frederic's card, which was
half in English and half in Russian. On the
other side she read a stylish cursive writing,

*Dear Jaden Steele, How are you? It
would be my honor to see you. Could we
dine together? Please call the Hotel
Monterey at your convenience. Sincerely,
Frederic Melnikov.*

Jaden stared at the card. He had added
the hotel's number and his room number.
The first thing she decided was that Frederic
was not grief stricken about Igor Kurloff's
murder. He could have a motive. The dancer
was the ballet's artistic director. He and Igor
could have clashed. Now she had the chance
to call him at the hotel. Her eyes darted from
the card to the phone and back again. She sat
back in her chair and gazed out the window
into the court, over to the empty display
window of the gallery. For a moment, just a
moment, disappointment made her heart feel

heavy. Why should she feel disappointed? Think of how much the sale meant to Gene and Bill. And William "Aram" Amirkhanian lived upstairs. He could paint more. She should feel happy for both of them.

Bill's paintings had a quality that drew her into them. Was she the only one who noticed this effect? Maybe it was her own imagination at work.

Jaden had read reviews of his paintings that never mentioned that quality.

She could escape into his scenes as she could escape into a good novel. In one of her favorite childhood books, Mary Poppins, the characters jumped into sidewalk chalk paintings, into another world that came alive. Today people can jump into a virtual computer world. In fact, she thought that too many young people lived in cyberland instead of in real life.

Hal broke into her thoughts. "Does that dancer want a date with you?"

"I think he does."

"Take care, Jaden."

That much she had already figured out by herself. "Aren't you the same Hal who was just telling me earlier to take chances?"

Hal shook his head. "Don't remind me. Yes, I did. Now you must be careful."

Jaden's mind raced. *I could find out more by going out with him than Bill could with a day of questioning.* Temptation and burning curiosity overwhelmed her. She picked up the phone. Frederic was not in his room. She left a message.

Hal moved to the desk. "Jaden," He spoke in a quiet but forceful tone,

"Don't go anywhere with Frederic without telling one of us where."

"You're right, Hal. Please don't worry about me. With all of you I have the best family of guardian angels that anyone could imagine." She surprised herself with the realization that these people she had known barely a year were like a family. A wildly interesting family.

Eclectic bunch, but more interesting than everyone being exactly alike.

Hal said with a smile, "You are a big girl, Jaden. It's getting quiet. Time to close. By the way, save that note. The signatures of famous people can be valuable, after all. Plus, it's a personal note."

"I may frame it someday." *If Frederic was not a murderer.* "I'll check the day's receipts and make certain everything is on the computer. You go home, Hal."

"Only if I lock the door."

"Fine. Thanks, Hal." She slipped on her glasses. "I'll see you Saturday."

Jaden concentrated on the excellent day's receipts. "If we keep this up, I can pay my bills." Hal was giving all of the businesses in the court a break on their leases. She had already discovered that most of the businesses in Carmel paid more than the residents of Dolores Court. Because she had purchased the business from Hal, she probably had the best terms on her lease. Hal had told her that nothing looked worse than an empty store.

She set the alarm and locked the door. In the court Kyle waved to her. "Are you as exhausted as we are?" he called. She nodded, her foot on the first step of the stairs. Each step felt as though it was ten feet higher than the next.

She blinked. Bill was walking down the steps. Though his face was still pale, he looked fit and handsome in that dark blue uniform. He did not smile.

"Hello, Jaden." He paused two steps above her. His pale face made his dark eyes appear black.

"Hello, Bill. Did you get enough rest?"

"Not really. It will take me a couple of days to catch up. Going in to dinner?"

"Right. A sandwich if I can put it together. And after that a hot shower and blessed bed."

His dark eyes sparkled as he said quietly, "Sleep tight."

From her perch on top of the stair post, Arizona nudged her. Jaden stroked the cat's soft white head while she watched Bill walk quickly down the last three steps. He turned left at the entrance of the court to walk up the three blocks to the police station at Junipero and Fourth Streets.

Jaden trudged the few steps to her own apartment. An omelet sounded better than a sandwich. She had not eaten anything since their large breakfast early in the morning. The dull headache that had persisted during the day turned into a deep throb. She pulled butter, two eggs, a tomato and some jack cheese from the refrigerator. Everything seemed to be an effort but the butter and eggs finally sizzled in the pan. Just as she flipped the omelet over, the phone rang.

She pulled the pan off the heat and answered. "Hello."

"Hello. This is Jaden Steele?" came the familiar voice with the slight accent.

"Yes, Frederic. Hal Lamont gave me your card. Could I help you with something? It is a tragic time for your dance company."

"Jaden Steele, everyone is heartsick. Nicolas is in a rage. We do not know what will happen to our schedule. The police want to speak to some of us again. I've told everything I know."

Have you?

"I am so sorry. Is there something any of us can do?" She could not have left a broader opening.

"Yes," he answered. "Would you share a meal with me? This hotel is a lonely place."

"Are there members of your company who would like to share a dinner with us?"

She hesitated. The hotel must be full of dancers, Russian speaking dancers, who could keep him company. He has singled her out. She could not decline the opportunity. Her curiosity mushroomed. *Am I making a big mistake?* The answer was no doubt *yes.*

"No," Frederic continued. "I do not believe that would be…good…my wishes. My wishes are to tell you something important."

"Right." Jaden already planned how to fend him off. In spite of that unnatural red hair, he was gifted with a magnetism that was extremely attractive. Like Boris and all the other male dancers, pure muscle over bone. If he turned out to be an aggressive person, she would be no competition for his strength.

Should she take one of her knives? No, but if he were a killer….

"Are you free now?" Frederic asked.

"No, Frederic. Not tonight. I'm exhausted. How about tomorrow? I will come to your hotel and then we can walk to somewhere on the wharf."

"That would be excellent. I am also tired. We dancers need exercise for our muscles. We do not want to burden Nicolas. There is an exercise room in the hotel. We are practicing and doing weightlifting there. Also there is a sports center close. The police asked us not to go places alone."

You got some exercise walking around Carmel, Jaden thought, but she said, "That is good, Frederic. I will come tomorrow evening at six. We can walk from your hotel to a restaurant."

"I will be honored, Jaden Steele."

She hung up thinking about how she must be more than slightly crazy to meet with him. Bill would be furious. Frederic might or might not say anything important. She knew how William Aram would feel about her meeting the ballet star alone. She would not dare be honest and tell him that she was playing detective again. That burning curiosity was part of her nature that Jaden knew could not be extinguished. Even now the names of the Kurloff Dancers whirled through her mind. Olga, Larissa, Tanya, Maria, Yelena, and Nina were in the sugar plum dance sequence with Frederic. There were three other male dancers whose names she could not remember. Boris danced the part of Drosselmeyer. There was the backstage crew and Nicolas. She needed to look at the program to refresh her memory. *Something seriously wrong in the relationship between Igor and his wife that deserved investigation.* A strong motive. Now Tatiana was free.

Nicolas could have murdered his brother. *Cain and Abel.* The more she thought about that, the more she felt certain that Nicolas was genuinely horrified by Igor's death. Less feelings and more facts, she told herself.

Jaden went to bed planning the best way to talk to Frederic about the Kurloff's relationship. He would know. The company dancers lived and traveled together for months, years. Frederic was the type who would know everyone's story.

With only a slight hesitation, she pulled open the door of her nightstand and reached under some papers for her small torsion assisted Monarch knife. Tonight it felt just as comfortable as when her husband had given it to her. Brent had it custom tailored for her hand. She closed her eyes and felt his lips brush her fingertips before he surprised her with the redwood handled beauty. "It's made for you, Jaden. The Monarch butterflies are faithful travelers. Steady on their course, like you."

You have such long, graceful fingers, my love. She heard his voice echo in the quiet bedroom. *Jaden, watch out!* She gasped.

A lump stuck in her throat.

She shook her head and opened her eyes.

Jaden slipped the Monarch into her small evening bag. There was little else to do for protection. She had not practiced in weeks. *Could I practice sometime tomorrow?* As long as she felt the familiar handle, Jaden knew she would never lose her touch. From the moment her grandfather put the handle of one of his own knives in her hand, Jaden felt a kinship with the hand carved bone, the sharp blade, and all of her ancestors. It was not a talent a young girl normally exhibited. She wondered if only the men had done knife throwing in Europe. Her gypsy ancestors used knife throwing to raise money. She could ask Bobbi to look that up for her. A good reference librarian should love a question like that. Jaden slipped under the down quilt, thinking of those hours spent with her grandfather throwing knives.

"Clear your mind. Focus, little one." His voice came to her as clearly as when she was seven years old.

Her grandmother protested, "Abel, this is not what little girls do!" Grandma lost the argument. Jaden had, by some joke of heredity, inherited every knife throwing gene from her grandfather's Roma ancestors. Throwing came as easily to her as running or drawing or playing a musical instrument came to others. Grandpa Abel never concealed his delight at her abilities. To compete with him, Grammy Ethel bought her dolls and they had tea parties together. Those miniature toy cups and saucers seemed dull compared to handling the knives.

The telephone's shrill ring split into her restless nightmare where red blood splashed around her like a series of waves beating on the shore. Forcing open one eye, she squinted at the clock while fumbling for the bedside phone. *Seven-thirty!* And with no problem at all she could have slept two or three hours more or maybe all day. Every joint in her body ached.

"Jaden." Bobbi's deep-toned voice was immediately recognizable.

"Morning, Bobbi," she answered in a husky voice as though she might be getting a cold. She cleared her throat.

"Jaden, I'm sorry. I woke you. I wanted to catch you before opening the store."

"Come over. Have you had breakfast?"

"Yes, but I would love some coffee. I have some information for you."

Jaden threw on her robe and headed for the kitchen to grind the blend from The Mad Hatters that she guessed must be mainly Kona coffee.

A whiff of the grind perked her up. "I need to cut back on this stuff."

She started the drip pot and ran to the bedroom to slip on some black wool slacks and a white pullover with Merry Christmas stamped across the front. 'Tis the season. I'd better wear this now. After Christmas I'll give the shirt away." Who would want it post-holiday?

"There is a home for everything," she heard Grandma Ethel speak from her childhood memories.

A soft knock on the door interrupted her high fashion consultation with herself.

As she was opening the door, Jaden realized she had forgotten to look through the peephole. Edward and Bill had both warned her to be careful. Who else could it be except for Bobbi?

Bill was standing there, glaring. "You didn't look through the viewer."

Jaden took a step backward in surprise.

Bill's gaze swept from her rumpled hair to the tips of her fuzzy pink slippers.

Her face reddened. He must see the guilt she was feeling. Could she get rid of him before her fellow sleuth came over from the next apartment?

Bill's face softened. "Merry Christmas to you, too. That coffee smells great."

Though she groaned to herself, Jaden asked, "Would you like some?"

"Thanks," he said, stepping in.

"Sit down." She pointed to the table pulling three mugs from the cupboard and filled one for him. "Sugar? Milk?"

"No, thanks. Black. Your coffee smells wonderful. What brand is it?"

"It's the Hawaiian blend that Sydney originated. They order a fifty pound sack and let me buy some. They told me they went through a hundred blends before they found *the one*."

"Sounds just like Syd." Bill sipped his coffee "They should patent it. You are certainly a favorite with the owners of *The Mad Hatters*."

"I asked about their coffee one day because I loved the flavor. That's why the favoritism. They asked me to keep quiet about selling it to me. Mine never seems quite as good as theirs." She gave him a quick smile.

"Maybe because someone else is brewing it. Like when other people's cooking always tastes better. Are you expecting someone else?" Bill nodded toward the two mugs by the coffeepot.

"As a matter of fact, I thought you were Bobbi. Sometimes we have breakfast together before work."

"I won't keep you then, Jaden. I'm sorry. I'm actually interviewing people."

"Why?" Her heart accelerated. "Is it still the murder or is something else wrong?"

His dark eyes stared directly into hers. "When did you last see Gene Miller?"

She should answer him as honestly as she could. *The empty display window in the gallery. He had a buyer that he wanted to meet. A sale would be important.*

"I saw him sitting on a bench in First Murphy Park." *Please. I hope he's all right.*

A knock at the door saved her temporarily from more explanations.

Bobbi came into the room carrying one of her numerous manila folders. When Bobbi saw Bill, even the poker-faced librarian could not hide her feelings. She looked as though she had been caught robbing a bank.

Jaden thought her own shirt might have read "guilty" instead of Merry Christmas.

"Morning coffee klatch, am I right?" Bill's voice contained more than a hint of sarcasm. He gulped his coffee. "If I can't cure you two, please at least be careful."

"I'm writing a book," Bobbi lied. "My life story. Notorious gets one a lot of money. There's nothing people like better than gossip and wild behavior. Sex sells."

She was digging herself a big hole. The last thing Bobbi wanted was publicity.

Bill stared at her until she finally turned her expressive golden-flecked eyes away.

He knew she was lying.

Jaden said, "Bill was asking about the last time we saw Gene."

"Yesterday morning," she said honestly, glancing briefly at Jaden. "Why are you asking? What's happened?"

Jaden knew they should tell him about Frederic and Gene.

Bill answered, "His car was parked on 11th in Pacific Grove all night. It was towed. I could not reach him by phone. And I noticed that my painting of Carmel Beach is gone from the gallery window. He told me he might have a buyer. It wasn't in the car. We checked at the impound lot."

"The gallery was closed yesterday. That's very unusual," Jaden said.

"It is. Gene rarely closes. His expenses are high. People have less money now for luxuries so a sale is a sale." A deep frown knotted Bill's forehead. "Doesn't sound like him at all. There's a possibility it could have been an elaborate robbery scheme. I'm worried that something happened to him. He is not answering his cell phone."

"He said he had an appointment with someone who was interested in your seascape that was in the gallery window. Could there be a connection between Igor's murder and Gene's disappearance?" Jaden whispered her last speculation. There had to be a connection.

"If he is all right, he's going to be mad to hear that his car is in Salinas. If I had known earlier, I could have brought the car back with me, but it was too late by the time they called our station."

"Gene would never have done that," Bobbi protested. "Something's wrong."

"That's what I thought, too. And every time he has an appointment about one of my paintings, he calls me with every detail. I did not hear a word all day yesterday. Of course, because of the murder, he could easily have forgotten and I was really busy."

Jaden knew that because of their sudden silence, the three of them were thinking the same thing. Now would be the time for her to tell Bill what she had seen yesterday.

She exchanged a look with Bobbi. For a moment neither of them said a word.

The librarian spoke first, "Gene would never leave the gallery like that. Those paintings are his whole life. He's a workaholic. Jaden, could it be that the famous Frederic Melnikov is a killer?"

"When I saw him in the park, he was sitting with Frederic. It does not seem possible that he could be responsible for the murder and is a kidnapper, too. There's a giant piece of this puzzle missing."

"More than one piece." When Bobbi half-closed her eyes, they became more slanted. That meant that she was thinking deeply, almost in a half dreamy state. She was trying to assemble the facts, too, into some pattern or picture that they could recognize. That way they could fit in the next piece. The empty space looked like a black hole

"You two are playing detective. Haven't I warned you about this?" Bill glared at each of them in turn. Jaden blinked first.

His last words to them as he left were, "Stay out of this, ladies."

Jaden and Bobbi stared at each other.

Finally Bobbi said, "I'll keep checking their backgrounds."

I should have told both of them about my date with Frederic

Since the distance to the Monterey Hotel on Alvarado Street from the bay was so short, she parked the car at the wharf and walked up two blocks in the now dark evening. She never got used to night descending at five p.m. in the winter. Walking helped her clear her mind. From the boats at the harbor to almost every store she passed, holiday light decorations twinkled or blinked.

The unmistakable dancer was already standing outside the downtown hotel. This place was certainly less expensive than the many motels in the city and on Cannery Row, but it had been revamped so it was a pleasant, convenient place to stay.

Everything was walking distance. The company no doubt received a group rate by booking most of the entire three story hotel.

"Jaden!" Frederic greeted her like a long lost sister. His muscular arms engulfed her. "I am so glad that you came to me!"

Once she recovered from her surprise at the warm welcome, Jaden pulled back a little. "It is nice to see you again, Frederic. How are the company members doing?"

Frederic's smile vanished. His silent stare down at the sidewalk said everything.

Jaden glanced into the small lobby and noticed several company members staring at them. By tomorrow everyone in the hotel would know about their meeting. "We will walk down to the wharf. Do you think anyone else would like to come with us?"

"No." He took her arm as he obviously wanted to quickly escape the gaze of his fellow company members. "Let them be envious of us."

They walked across the wharf parking lot past the first building by the water.

"That's the old customs house." Jaden pointed. "It's an historical monument. Monterey was the first capital of California. There are many historic buildings here. You could take a walking tour because they are all around you in the downtown."

"My homeland has many historical sites," Frederic responded.

Of course, the age of Russian historic sites might be ten times what was built in Monterey in the nineteenth century. "This is a much younger country," she commented. "Do you have a *Walking Through History Brochure?* Bobbi can bring you one from the library. Your hotel is in an excellent location for walking tours of the city."

Frederic nodded. "Monterey is a beautiful sight. The colored lights from the boats reflect on the water. And you being here make it more beautiful."

Jaden felt momentarily awed by the dancer's captivating charm. The barking of the sea lions in the yacht harbor snapped her back to reality. "Why, thank you, Frederic."

"You are very welcome. I see many restaurants here. Is there one you favor?"

"My favorite is the *Captain's Table.*"

"Then we shall attend there."

When they reached the restaurant, he graciously opened the door for her. Since it was not the weekend, they were seated by the window where the lights on all of the boats played on the dark, still water. An artificial but brilliantly lit tree gave the Captain's Table a holiday flair.

The waiter asked, "Would you like to start with a drink?"

Jaden said, "I'd like a glass of Brassfield sauvignon blanc, please."

"Thank you," Frederic said. "A coke."

The waiter nodded and left.

Frederic must have thought she needed an explanation. "I do not drink. My father killed himself with vodka. Too common in my country. And I do believe that it is bad for dancers. Athletes must keep their bodies in perfect condition."

"I understand, Frederic."

"It is very hard for a family when someone drinks too much. One thing easy to find in Russia is vodka. Other countries, too. Often half of the men are drinkers. Did you know that?"

"No, I didn't." *Could that be true?*

He went on, "Very hard on a young boy but my strong mother did the best she could for us. All she wanted to do was escape. She dreamed of taking us to America. Her sister was already here." There was obvious pain in Frederic's dark eyes as he spoke. "My father died of the disease that kills drinkers. The liver dies and then the body."

Jaden nodded. A lump in her throat kept her from saying anything.

Frederic went on, "My mother died young, too. She never came to the United States. I was but sixteen when she finally died. Someday, I told myself, I will see this America of people's dreams."

"It must have been a difficult time."

"Yes, a very sad time. But my mother saw to it that I trained as a dancer. I was accepted by a dance company in our city. They gave me a home."

Jaden's wine arrived.

"What would you like?" The waiter asked with his pencil poised for their orders.

"I'll have the locals' special, calamari, green salad and Italian dressing," she said.

"I will have the same," Frederic told him. When the waiter left, he spoke with a soft smile, "Skol, Jaden Steele." He lifted his glass of coca-cola.

She noticed a couple at the table across from theirs had been staring at them. Finally, the man came over to their table. "Excuse me. We could not help recognizing Mr. Melnikov. Sir, my wife would so love to meet you. She is a great fan of the ballet."

"Certainly," Frederic smiled graciously.

The man nodded to his wife who got up and came to their table. The woman's face visibly reddened as she was introduced.

Frederic rose. "I am honored." He bowed his head and took the woman's hand, kissing it while the woman looked as though she was going to collapse.

"May I introduce my companion, Jaden Steele?" Frederic said.

The couple shook hands with her.

"We won't intrude anymore," the man told them. "It was such a pleasure."

They returned to their table talking excitedly about the meeting.

She heard the woman whispering, "He is as attractive as I've heard."

Jaden was reminded of Frederic's reputation as a heartthrob in those tabloids that shouted at you from the market checkout stands. Photographers had well recorded his dates with several movie and television leading ladies. He must be the most well-known of the Kurloff Company. Now they were speculating on who she was.

"You were very gracious with the woman, Frederic. They are fans."

He nodded, smiling. "It takes little effort to be nice to those people who support the arts. And I like ladies and was well taught to please them by the prima ballerina of my first ballet company."

"You were taught?" Jaden felt her eyebrows lift in surprise. *Well, why not?*

"Yes. My friend taught me what to say to women to flatter them. She taught me how to be a good lover."

The frankness made Jaden's fork pause over her salad. Her mind whirled with the realization that the man could no doubt back up everything he said. She forced the tines into a tomato, thinking that his proposition was coming early in the evening.

"Really?"

"Yes, she was married to an eighty year old German businessman. She liked me and taught me how to please women in all ways. And I was young and eager. Her husband cared for her in his own way and understood that she needed the lovers."

Jaden almost fell off her chair when she thought of his age. "You were seventeen."

"She was my excellent teacher to the age of twenty-one. She did not love me. The prima ballerina was fond of me. At first I was so young and so excited about what I thought was love. Later I realized the physical relationship was not love."

Jaden decided to be just as direct, "You think she took advantage of an orphaned young man?"

"Of course. My mother certainly would not have permitted our affair. It was a fortunate way to learn, though. As a young man I thought the physical sex was all. There is so much more. I have never failed to please, though women are very complicated. Often they want me to commit to a relationship."

A busboy brought the main course.

Every once in a while, the woman across the way shot Jaden an envious glance.

"My friend always knew what she was doing. She openly admitted marrying the older man for his money. He greatly admired her. His sexual drive was gone but he did lust for status. He offered that when he died she would be very wealthy. The man had given her a lot of money to marry him. Fate plays grim tricks. She found that she had cancer and died about age forty. Two years later he died."

Jaden was surprised to feel sorry for this woman who obviously planned her life well from marrying a wealthy old husband to taking several young lovers. Fate can be a grim joker.

She dug into her calamari steak.

"This is delicious," Frederic commented. "You have made a great evening. Thank you, Jaden Steele. There is something I must tell you and I have waited too long."

Jaden braced herself for a proposition. He no doubt was a good lover. Curiosity was getting the better of her. She forced herself to look stoic.

"When I first saw you at your store, I recognized something. During that long night after Igor's murder, I realized you have a quality very much like my mother's."

Jaden groaned to herself. Her fork slipped out of her hand and fell on her almost empty plate. She was prepared for anything but being compared to someone's mother. She was surprised to feel a wave of disappointment washing over her.

"I had always good rapport with my mother. I knew I could confide in you."

Confide in me? Just what's wrong with me? *His mother!* Scolding herself, Jaden snapped back to reality. This is why she agreed to going out with the dancer in the first place.

Fine detective she made just because her ego took a hit.

Frederic leaned over his dinner to whisper, "Jaden, there is great danger here."

"Certainly. The person who murdered Igor Kurloff is violent. You don't have to mention that there is danger. Can you explain more?"

Frederic sat back and looked down at his half eaten calamari and rice. "I cannot explain to you right now. I had hoped that you would speak to your friend, William. The one who is a policeman. He is also your very good friend. I noticed the way he looked at you when we were in the auditorium. Often he looks at you with love. Do you know?"

She stared at her plate.

Jaden knew Bill liked her. If it were that obvious to strangers, she needed to be more careful when she dated him, or maybe she should not go out with him at all.

"Can it be that you are surprised about your friend who would like to be more than a friend?" Frederic asked.

He could have been the communication teacher. Except for that vague threat of danger, the man's personality appeared to be open and direct.

"No." Jaden shook her head. "I know he is my friend. I like him."

"Friends? You are not lovers? Do you realize that he desires you?" Frederic asked.

Jaden felt her face grow hot. The dancer was finding out more about her than she was about him. And also playing matchmaker. Bill almost always seemed moody and distant around her. He often reminded her of black gathering clouds before a thunderstorm. She thought the moodiness was his artistic temperament. Now she felt his behavior might be because he did not want to be rejected. And she felt certain he was like Frederic, rarely rejected. Women probably pursued the dancer.

Frederic possessed keen insight and an unusual amount of frankness because he was so confident in himself. Since he was a world famous star he could also say what came to his mind without fearing his audience. People would want to stay on his good side. Even his unique honesty was in a way very attractive.

Jaden definitely wanted to change their conversation, and her own senses told her that Frederic knew more than he was saying. She asked, "Can you tell me anymore? what do you know about the gallery owner, Gene Miller? That's the art gallery across from my shop. You saw it yesterday. Bill is worried about him. His car was found parked overnight on 11th in Pacific."

The sudden question made him fumble for words. "The art gallery across from your store? Gene Miller runs the business. Are you certain that the man has disappeared?"

He was stalling and Jaden knew it by the way his expressive body moved. She kept on, "The police are looking for him."

"That is sad." For a second she imagined that a smile flickered across his face. "America is a dangerous country." His eyes darted to the water. A playful sea lion took that moment to splash up through the dark water right by their window. Everyone seated near them turned to look through the large plate glass to the harbor.

Jaden knew Frederic was not telling the truth. She decided he certainly knew Gene.

Once they finished their cannelloni and coffee Frederic paid their bill and they walked outside on the wharf. The barking of the sea lions drowned out the traffic noises. Jaden took Frederic to the railing to see about twenty of the ocean mammals in their perches under the wharf. Frederic stared across the water. "This is a beautiful place."

How quickly and obviously he changed the subject from dangerous to beautiful.

"Yes, the setting is beautiful. Even in storms, watching the ocean is fascinating. Bill has done a painting of a stormy Carmel Beach in winter. It is one of my favorites. And at Asilomar beach the waves crash dangerously on the dark rock shelves. I can't describe the haunting beauty of the point. There are surfers. Few people actually go into the water." Jaden's mind raced back to the missing gallery owner with Bill's missing and valuable painting. He and the oil were certainly together.

Gene would go almost anywhere for a sale. Her instinct told her that Frederic was being unusually vague and certainly calm about the news of the disappearance.

Since he did not appear to be upset about someone vanishing that he obviously knew; it must mean that he knew the reason.

Am I depending on my hunches too much? Jaden remembered Conan Doyle's larger than life Sherlock Holmes.

Whatever is left after you eliminate everything else must be the truth. But what or who can I eliminate? There were too many people.

"Frederic," she began slowly but suddenly changed her mind, "do you know anything about why Gene would disappear or where he went?"

He stared at her. Then he turned back to look at the water. "Jaden, forgive me but I did want to give you warning of the danger. Will you arrange some way for me to see your friend? After that, I will explain to you." Without warning he moved forward to take her by both shoulders. His hands were strong and she knew there was little chance for her to twist away. She thought of the Monarch knife, which rested uselessly in the bottom of her evening bag. His gaze felt intense. "Please take care, Jaden. I do not mean to put you in any danger. You will promise me?"

She nodded, unable to respond.

He pulled her close with his strong arms and kissed her.

All Jaden could hear was the booming of her own heart. She almost forgot where she was and the information she was supposed to be gathering.

Frederic pulled away gently and said, "You are a beautiful woman, Jaden Steele."

Jaden could not catch her breath. For a moment she would have gone anywhere with him just to see if his reputation was as real as she imagined.

He slipped his hand into hers as they walked across the wharf to the parking lot.

"If someone is watching," he whispered, "they must believe we are romantic."

"That we are having a romantic evening." Jaden corrected him without thinking. But in several ways it really had been a romantic evening. She still felt confused about his warnings and bristled about "reminding him of his mother" but was truly fascinated by the superb dancer. By her own reaction to him, she had no doubts about what he said openly, that he was a good lover. He had a practiced way of making a woman feel important. His not explaining what he meant by the danger was out of character. What was he holding back?

"Frederic, why will you not tell me who or what is the danger?"

He did not answer as they were walking along the boardwalk. The bright lights of the restaurants and the gift shops distracted her for the short walk to the parking lot.

This silence from someone she knew could speak very well could mean that she was "having an exciting, romantic evening" with a killer.

Out of the corner of her eye, she noticed an old woman, shopping cart piled high, going through a garbage can. The bag lady was about twenty-five feet away very near her car.

Oh, no, it can't be, Jaden thought. Bobbi the chameleon would not follow me without saying anything, or would she? Bobbi could be secretive. Between Bobbi and Edward she was not certain....

Bobbi had done it before. Jaden knew that because retired Intelligence General Edward Stennis recognized and encouraged her talent for disguises, The librarian plunged right into being a chameleon.

"I went from being notorious Petra Jones-Schmidt to being invisible," she told Jaden. "Any time you want me to be someone else, let me try."

Bobbi played the bag lady part that terrifying evening when Marian Panetti entered the shop to kill Jaden. The "old woman" distracted Marion long enough for Jaden to save her own life.

As they neared the car, Jaden pressed the remote to "unlock." Frederic held the driver's door for her and sprang around to the passenger's side. Out of curiosity, Jaden suddenly decided to flick on her brights. The flash of unexpected light made the bag lady jump. She moved around and in back of the trash can away from the parking lot lights to the relative safety of the night shadows.

Frederic gasped. He suddenly leaned close to the windshield, staring.

If that woman is Bobbi, Jaden thought, *I'm going to tell her that I'm not very happy about being followed anonymously.*

But she had not told Bobbi about her date with Frederic. And she had forgotten Hal's warning. Jaden drove out of the near empty lot and up Alvarado Street to the Monterey Hotel. She pulled to the curb thinking of what she had learned about the famous dancer's background and love life.

A book about his life would be a best seller. Frederic continued to stare out the windshield. "You will tell Bill to call me?" Frederic reminded her in a quiet but slightly shaky voice.

"Yes, I understand how important it is. First thing in the morning. Frederic, are you all right?"

Ignoring her question he opened the car door and stepped out to the curb. "This has been a delightful evening. Thank you, Jaden Steele." He suddenly spoke in a voice unnecessarily loud.

A sudden blinding series of flashes made Jaden cover her eyes.. Her heart thumped and finally slowed to a steady beat. She felt certain this was the bag lady's revenge. *Photographers*.

"Do not be afraid. Someone is taking pictures. The paparazzi have been slow to arrive but now they are here. Several company members have already been interviewed for television. They asked me if I would be available for interviews. Normally I enjoy the interviews but I do not wish to speculate on Igor's murder. Jaden, best you leave quickly."

More flashes went off around them. Jaden groaned. *They've got some great pictures of my car. Some detective I am!*

"Good night, Frederic."

The Monterey Police Department did not issue a news bulletin until last night. Now the news reporters would be around in force and especially around Frederic who never discouraged them.

A picture of her car with Frederic standing next to it flashed across her mind. The national tabloids would love the story. Jaden knew how much Bobbi despised her own notoriety. Few people knew that she moved to Carmel and she wanted to keep it that way. Jaden did not want to be the news of the week. And she certainly did not want even accidentally to put Bobbi back in the news. There was nothing she could do about what had already happened.

I have to be more careful, even if I have to learn to disguise myself. Jaden wondered if she dared ask Bobbi to help her.

Jaden wondered if it were possible to disguise herself. Some people had the talent.

Maybe everyone is acting.

All the world's a stage.

The drive back to Carmel on Carpenter Street took fifteen minutes. She must call Bill first thing in the morning. He would not like learning about her dinner with Frederic. She would explain it as a simple date. She actually went for information. Jaden suspected that Frederic might know the identity of the murderer even if he did not realize it.

She always hated going into the parking garage where Sergio was murdered.

Although she drove up and down the divided Junipero Street twice, all of the spaces were full. Jaden headed to the driveway entrance under the court. She pressed the automatic gate opener.

Another person she would call would be her librarian friend. She felt like going over tonight to see if Bobbi were home. Actually, Jaden thought with a smile as she picked up her cell phone, this is one way to find out.

To her complete surprise, Bobbi answered right away. "Hello."

Jaden cleared her throat, "Bobbi? Ahhh… this is Jaden."

"Where are you? Are you all right?"

"Yes. I'm in the parking garage. You know how much this place frightens me at night. Would you mind coming down?"

"I understand. I'll be right down."

In a few minutes Bobbi, bearing no resemblance to a bag lady, appeared at the bottom of the stairway. Edward Stennis stood behind her.

He must have been with her, Jaden thought, dismissing the fact that someone else might be having a romantic evening. Edward was a full thirty years older than Bobbi. Anything was possible. Frederic said that his friend married an eighty year old for his money and quite honestly admitted it. Well, that was not the first time in history.

145

"I'm glad you were home," Jaden said sheepishly, wanting to apologize for her suspicious thoughts.

"That's all right. You can count on us any time," Edward answered. "Call any of us. Someone's bound to be home. We understand perfectly how you feel."

"Thanks, Edward. I feel a little like a baby. If I could have found a place in the all night spaces on the street, I would have." The beep from the automatic lock echoed in the small concrete garage.

"Did you go out with Bill?" Bobbi asked as they walked up the stairs and crossed the court to the steps to the second floor. For a few seconds she thought she saw a statue on the top post, but the statue moved to greet them. Arizona liked to follow everyone up and down the stairs. The cat took her guard dog status seriously.

"Let's go into my apartment first. Is it too late for coffee for you?"

She unlocked the door and the three of them entered her living room.

Jaden explained the dinner with Frederic, detail by detail. When she deliberately set out to remember scenes, her mind was even sharper.

"Frederic warned you about some danger?" Edward asked. "It's a little after the fact. Did he say anything more than that?

It is obvious that someone who can be very deadly is running around."

Jaden poured coffee for them. Decaf for Bobbi. "He was quite serious. He wants to speak to Bill as soon as possible. He wanted to tell Bill, but not me. What did you find out about him, Bobbi?"

"Not too much. His mother died when he was fifteen, almost sixteen. He was hired by the St. Petersburg Ballet and worked there until he went to work for the Kurloffs. He's very charming. Always a favorite with women. Frederic is always friendly to the press so he's a favorite with them, too. I must have looked at fifty pictures of him with beautiful women. And not one of them ever complained. He's been interviewed on television, radio, for dance magazines and for fan magazines."

Edward spoke quietly. "Let me try."

Even retired, General Stennis had contacts for more information than probably most people in government. Once he was through with his investigation, there would be nothing secret about the famous man.

"I wanted to try some of the genealogy web sites to trace his family," Bobbi sipped her decaf.

"You do that and I will try my way."

"Do you think he could be the murderer?" Bobbi asked. "There was a break when he was offstage."

"It is hard to believe. He does have the strength. Frederic seems open and honest." Jaden smiled for a brief moment and decided not to go over the good lover conversation. "He seemed very concerned about the danger. That was the first time in the evening that he refused to be pinned down. The same with Gene Miller's disappearance. I suspected he knew something about it, especially after seeing him with Gene in First Murphy Park."

"Jaden, you have great instincts," Edward commented. "I'll find out everything possible about him from birth and before."

"There's a biography about him in the library. I'll start reading that."

Jaden wanted to ask Bobbi about being a bag lady. Finally she realized that the chameleon would have had to fly over here and remove her make-up and clothes in, what? Under twenty minutes? Not impossible but unlikely. *The old woman she and Frederic had seen was just some poor old bag lady.*

"There's another thing," Jaden began. "I think my car is going to be news tomorrow. The photographers are in Monterey now.

They love Frederic. When I let him off at the hotel, several people took his picture."

"Ohhh," Edward groaned. "That's bad if anyone can recognize your car or read the license plate. If there is danger you are going to be right in the middle of it. The news of the murder is exploding in the media. Maybe you should stay with Bobbi or my mother for awhile."

"I don't want to do that," Jaden answered. "At least I have until tomorrow morning before the papers come out. The net is 24/7."

"Someone could have followed you here." Bobbi took her mug to the sink.

Jaden called Bill first thing in the morning. She invited him for breakfast hoping to soften what she would tell him about the evening with Frederic, and the fact that the dancer and Gene had been talking in the park just before the gallery owner disappeared. He should have been told.

"I'll be right over, Jaden." He sounded brighter than normal.

In sixty seconds he was knocking at the door. She peered through the viewer and then welcomed him in.

"I'm glad you looked through that peephole," he commented. He was freshly showered with his dark, damp hair slicked back. Bill could not have looked more attractive. He smiled.

"I'm going to fix eggs and toast for us, Bill. My food supply is low, not that it's ever large. I eat out at the Mad Hatter a lot. Please, sit down."

"Eggs and toast would be great. I could cook the eggs if you want."

"Just tell me how you like them." She poured orange juice for them.

"Sunny side up."

"That's a coincidence." One at a time, she broke three eggs into the sizzling butter. "That's how I like them."

Because she fried the eggs in butter, she decided to have dry toast for herself. Whether or not she was saving calories was debatable. The butter container and the raspberry jam went on the table for Bill to use if he wanted.

Once they were sitting down and beginning to eat, she took a sip of coffee to fortify herself. "Bill, I saw Frederic Melnikov last night."

He stopped eating and stared at her. "You saw him accidentally?"

"No. I had a date with him."

"A date?" He realized his voice was too loud for the small apartment. He lowered his tone. "A date?" *Just when he was thoroughly enjoying having breakfast with her. How does that guy rate anyway?* He chomped down on his toast. It broke in his hand and cascaded onto his remaining eggs.

"For dinner. You're right about me. I'm too curious. He asked me. I was hoping to learn more about him and the company. I couldn't say no."

"You certainly could have said no. It's a simple one-syllable word."

"He did not invite me out on a real date." Her ego prevented her from saying that she thought it was a date. "He wants to see you as soon as possible. Frederic says there is danger. He was obviously afraid that if he contacted you directly someone in the company would find out."

"I'll call him right away." He took such a huge bite of his second piece of toast that only half of it was left.

"There's more." She closed her eyes and opened them, staring into his dark eyes.

She cleared her throat out of nervousness and began telling him about seeing Frederic and Gene in the park.

As she spoke, his brow furrowed. "You didn't think to tell me?" His cheekbones were reddening as he plainly tried to control his anger. "Bobbi and Esther and God knows who else knew? No doubt Esther told her son. Do you realize the danger? You might have been out with a murderer!"

"I don't think he's the murderer. But it did cross my mind."

"At least you thought that much! You can't always rely on 'feelings,' Jaden. I've met a lot of perfect liars."

She swallowed hard. Her instincts were usually correct. He was right, too. Because she felt guilty about not telling Bill, her face grew flushed. "I'm sorry about not telling you right away. I've been going over and over how to tell you because I knew you would not be happy."

"That's true." The two staccato words escaped his lips as he stood up. He took in a deep breath. "I'm going to call the dancer right now. Do you have the hotel's number and Frederic's room number?" *He had trouble staying angry with her, especially when she knew she had made a mistake.*

"By the phone," she answered softly.

Silently he took his plate to the sink and rinsed it off.

"I'll clean up," Jaden stood up.

He quickly dodged around her and went to read the notepad by the phone. "I ought to pick him up for police questioning, but I want to hear what he says first."

When it was obvious he was leaving, she said, "You can call him from here."

"No, I'm calling from my apartment. I may want a search warrant for his hotel room, although there is not much evidence." He headed for the door. Suddenly Bill halted and turned toward her, speaking in a steady, controlled voice, "Jaden, you do realize what danger you could have been in when you went out with Melnikov?"

She nodded, answering feebly, "I wanted to find out what I could from him."

Bill opened the door. "You have to stop diving into that curiosity pool of yours. Someday, something lurking in the water is going to pull you right under. No one will be around to help you."

Hot tears burned in Jaden's eyes.

He closed the door with a bang.

The tears came from being angry at herself for allowing him to tell her to mind her own business. Jaden had to admit to herself that the chance to go out with one of the world's most famous dancers and media personalities was also too tempting. She sank down onto the sofa, slowly recognizing that Bill was trying to boss her around because he wanted to protect her. Jaden was stubbornly resisting feelings for Bill that welled up inside of her. It was like trying to perfectly plan the next ten years of your life and getting hit by a truck.

I do not want to be involved with anyone right now. It's too soon after the disastrous affair with Sergio. How was it possible for me to be blind and stupid at the same time? Certainly her brief affair with Sergio Panetti proved that. I missed Brent so much. Sometimes she actually begged "Brent, please tell me what to do."

Now, here, is my new life. I will never jump into a relationship again.

Tears welled and spilled down her face. Jaden sank into the sofa, hugging a pillow. As her tears melted into the blue satin cushion, the realization that this was the first time she had cried since Brent's death hit her like an ocean wave. The kind woman police officer who came to tell her about the accident hugged Jaden while she sobbed uncontrollably. Her husband was gone.

"Is there someone I can call for you?" the officer had asked.

All of her family were gone, too. She asked the officer to call one of her friends at the University of Nebraska. Her lifetime friend, Mindy Porter, left her English class with a teaching assistant to come right over.

Those memories that Jaden thought she had buried proved so vivid that Brent's death might have been yesterday. Just when she thought the life shattering experience was fading it came to life. In frustration she flung the pillow at the door, stood up, and marched into the bathroom to splash cold water on her face.

Her knowledge of how guilty she was made a hard lump stick in her throat.

So I'll open the store with red eyes. She stared at her reflection in the mirror. Face powder did not mask those shiny red splotches on her face.

Petting fluffy Arizona at the top of the stairs made her feel slightly better. The cat went from statue to white lightning bolt in seconds when Jaden started down. The animal always took a haughty delight in beating Jaden downstairs. She sat at the bottom of the stairs, licking one paw and then the other until Jaden's shoes touched the flagstone courtyard. Then Arizona streaked back upstairs to the flat perch on the top railing to watch. She had even learned to sleep curled up on the flat top post. Unless the animal went into Esther's apartment, her main job duty was to survey her domain with those almond shaped half-closed golden-yellow eyes. The cat's eyes often functioned like mirrors. As far as

Jaden knew, Arizona was way too well fed to ever dream of hunting. He probably slept twenty-three hours a day.

Jaden punched in the alarm code and began the procedures to open the shop. It looked like she might need cash. Though most people paid by credit card there were always some who actually used old-fashioned United States mint products. As far as she knew, greenbacks were still made in the United States. She smiled remembering her grandfather selling meat and knives for *cash only*.

If someone he did not know wanted to pay by check, he made them go to the bank and cash it at the bank before he would part with a pound of hamburger. On the wall in back of grandpa were at least two dozen gleaming knives, any one of which he could snatch and throw in seconds. He stuck two bad checks to the center of a target painted on the wall with two of his own knives.

If someone argued about paying cash he would point and say, "I'm not striking out."

He always got the cash.

Grandpa Abel never owned a credit card. Society managed for eons without them.

She glanced up at the case on the wall facing Fifth Avenue that contained Grandpa's two now very valuable knives dwarfed by several even more valuable swords. A recent addition to the wall case had been a scythe with a gold plated handle that was supposed to have belonged to the king of some little country in Europe.

"They call it the 'Scythe of Death,' because legend says that the king presented it to a man who retired from his service as what one might today call a contract killer."

Hal told her about his internet purchase. "He farmed but occasionally was called back to consult with the tyrannical king about anyone who seemed to be giving him trouble. They would disappear. Then, one night, the scythe up and killed the farmer in revenge for being misused. About a month later the king, in spite of being well-guarded, was killed the same way. It may be a made-up legend to charge a high price for this thing, but I was hooked. The scythe is old and the plating real gold."

"You can't beat that story, Hal," Jaden shivered looking at the curved blade. "Now we just have to find someone else who believes it enough to buy the deadly-looking thing, someone with more money than critical thinking skills."

The bell tied to the front door rang. Jaden looked up with a start to see Bill standing in the shop. "I forgot to say something," he said quietly.

Jaden groaned to herself. Just when her eyes were returning to normal.

"I'll pick you up at seven tonight."

Jaden stared at him.

"The symphony concert at the Mission," he reminded her.

"Oh, I'd forgotten," Jaden almost whispered. Of course it was tonight.

Bill's eyes narrowed. "I'm not surprised that you forgot. I have the tickets. It's been a different week what with murders and disappearances, and secrets."

"Different is putting it mildly. I really am looking forward to the concert, Bill." She wondered if he noticed her splotchy face. Jaden sighed deeply. "The concert and the Mission church are always beautiful. I will be ready at seven." Jaden had been looking forward to the concert and could not believe she had forgotten.

He allowed a quick smile to cross his face before he said, "I spoke to your friend. We're going to have coffee at that little Russian café on the corner of Lighthouse and Eighteenth in Pacific Grove. He said he did not want to go anywhere near the hotel."

"He's afraid of someone," Jaden said. "I believe he knows what happened to Gene, and I know you must be thinking about what happened to both him and your beautiful Carmel River painting."

"The painting…I can bring life to a new canvas, Jaden. I could not do the same thing for Gene if something has happened to him. We need to find out where he is."

Bill placed his uniform in the trunk of his own car. Frederic asked him not to come as a police officer in case photographers followed him to the coffee shop. Bill hoped, like Jaden, that the ballet dancer would give him useful information. As he turned his car onto Fourth Avenue from Dolores, he realized that as curiosity went, he was no different than Jaden. He understood that part of her nature. He still could not control the fury that seethed inside because she had gone out with the man without telling him. In the store he knew she was still angry with him. Telling Jaden not to act on her curiosity was like telling the ocean not to have high tides. He knew he could not change her nature. *Because Jaden is such an expert with knives, she thinks she can take care of herself. She must learn to be careful.*

From Highway One he took the Munras exit to drive down Pacific toward the ocean. Once on Lighthouse Avenue he found a parking spot on a side street, Seventeenth, and walked a block to the café. The fresh ocean air filled his lungs and cleared his head. If their world had been trouble free, he would have liked to bring Jaden down here to walk along the beach trail and sit on a bench together to watch the ocean waves.

There were so many places along that walk that he could paint. He had placed Jaden in the painting that had disappeared with Gene. She was a small figure, painted from the back. No one would recognize her. Where is the painting now?

He was carrying on an unproductive conversation with himself. *In so many ways, my paintings are like my children.* It was completely out of character for Gene to disappear without a word and to leave the gallery closed. He always went over possible sale details with me. Bill dreaded the idea that something happened to his friend. As time went by, it seemed more and more likely. This was in no way his normal behavior. He could have been robbed.

A lump caught in Bill's throat. He was so lost in his thoughts that he did not realize that a man who was sitting on a bench at the bus stop rose to follow him to the café, a separate, 1940s-style stucco house with a second story apartment or apartments. The man pulled a San Francisco Giants baseball cap down over his forehead.

A sign in the window declared, "Russian pastries a specialty." A series of colorfully painted Russian nesting dolls, from the largest to the smallest, decorated the inside ledge of the plate glass window.

When Bill reached the entrance to the café, Mr. Giant's hat caught up with him.

"Sir?" the man held the door for him. Bill looked into his face and recognized the dancer, whose distinctive red hair was wisping out from under the cap.

"Frederic." They stepped into the shop. "That cap works really well," he commented. "I did not realize it was you until right now."

The dancer motioned to a booth in the very back of the crowded café.

The waitress said, "There's no window in that booth, gentlemen."

"That is fine. We do not wish to see the cars." He said it matter-of-factly and the waitress laughed. She handed them each a menu as they slipped into the brown leather booth. The cushions must have been newly recovered as their condition was excellent. They even smelled new.

"Coffee?" The waitress, Yessinia, asked.

"Thank you. This reminds me of a place in Fresno when I was a kid," Bill commented. "Most restaurants don't have booths any more. Did you see the Russian pastry? Is that why you found this place?"

"May I tell you something that you will not repeat? I believe that others may sooner or later find out. I wish to be as honest as possible with you."

Bill stared at him. "If you ask me not to repeat what you say, I will honor that, unless it has something to do with a crime."

"I do not believe it has anything to do with the murder." The two pairs of dark eyes met. "This is my house and business."

Bill almost fell off the edge of the booth. He shook his head. "Yours?"

"Yes. I inherited money. The United States does not restrict foreigners from owning property. Many countries do. About twelve years ago a relative told me what a beautiful area this was. I came here on a dance tour. My mother dreamed of coming to the United States. She would have been so happy to know that I bought property here. This building I could afford and purchased it. This was extremely fortunate. The price is now gigantic."

Bill could imagine. A corner building in Pacific Grove three blocks from the ocean. What would the price be today? Frederic was a free spirit even when he was young and certainly completely trained in socialist philosophy. In spite of that, he became a happy capitalist. Bill slowly processed this news and what it could mean.

Yessinia returned with coffee.

"The coffee is good," he commented. He set his cup down. "Twelve years ago you weren't very old. You inherited money?"

Frederic nodded. "Yes. Not from my parents, who both died very young, but from a good friend. I was sixteen when I was hired by the company where my friend was the prima ballerina. It was generous of her."

Bill pressed his back into the booth cushion. "A good friend."

"Yes. I do not mind telling you. Jaden knows. My friend was a ballerina who died before her time. Cancer. She liked me. Her husband knew. He was very old and very wealthy. Many Russians disliked her for marrying a German businessman, but she defied them. 'I do not wish to be a poor communist, and neither do you, if you will be honest with yourselves,' she told them flatly. "When my friend died, she left me a

166

hundred thousand American dollars. Her husband had no need for the money and did not object."

"Jaden knows this?" Bill shook his head.

"She does not know about the money. I told her about my friend, the prima ballerina. I do not think she approved. Her face is very expressive." Frederic's eyes twinkled as he watched Bill's reaction with a considerable amount of amusement.

"Her face is very expressive," Bill repeated in almost a whisper. He managed to control the quick smile that came to his lips. Usually it was easy to tell Jaden's feelings. Bobbi, though, controlled her facial reactions very well.

"You like her very much," Frederic said. "Have you told Jaden this?"

Bill opened his mouth to answer when he suddenly thought, who is questioning who here? Or is it whom? He clenched his teeth together not to snap that it was none of the dancer's business but decided to keep their first individual meeting as civil as possible. "I like Jaden." He responded casually but heard a slight tremor in his voice. He realized that his fingers were tightening on the handle of his coffee cup. He relaxed them.

"Then you should tell her. Women adore to hear that you like them above anyone else. Jaden is a beautiful woman. Many men would desire her."

Enough was enough. Bill swallowed hard and said, "Frederic, can you tell me what you know about Igor Kurloff's murder and Gene Miller's disappearance?"

The grin vanished from Frederic's face. "Someone in our company must have killed Igor. I am, what is the word? Nervous?"

"You don't know who?"

"What I do know is that the Kurloff's father was a KGB agent. If you are not familiar with Russia under the communists, it will be difficult for you to understand what the KGB was like. They are around today, I am sure."

"I only can imagine from stories that I have heard." He watched Frederic through the steam from his coffee. The dancer's brown eyes were steady, not shifting toward the table top or trying to avoid eye contact. Bill believed that he was telling the truth as he knew it. Criminals could fool him.

He felt Frederic was holding back.

"Communism was going to be the great salvation of the people. Everyone equal. It sounds logical, but it is one of history's jokes. Those who did not keep quiet were murdered. The easiest way to silence the opposition is to kill them. Party members took the important jobs. When I received money in a Swiss bank account, I quickly decided to buy property in the United States, property that would create an income. This is most capitalistic. My mother loved the idea of America. This building cost sixty thousand American dollars. Now worth two million dollars. I cannot dance forever so this property is like Aladdin's treasure. My mother dreamed of coming here to join her sister, but my aunt died."

He kept his eyes downcast, staring into his steaming coffee.

"In those days the defection of a famous performer was to be prevented by any means. We managed to keep the real estate purchase a secret."

Bill sipped his own, remembering phrases from his school days. *Exploited working class. Imperialists.*

At about age twenty the ballet dancer made an independent, unusual, highly intelligent choice.

Frederic went on, "Russian communism failed because it was a lie. The only people who prospered were privileged class members of the communist party. Officials got the best apartments, jobs. Fear kept people from protesting. I know this because my father also was a KGB agent."

Bill, conditioned to look for anything that was repetitive in a crime, heard KGB agent as though Frederic were shouting it. He did say, "But that was thirty years ago that he died."

"Memories remain. Many people wait years to exact revenge. Then probably Nicolas also was a KGB agent?"

"I believe so."

"They were acquainted with your father?" Note: Interview Nicolas again.

"Yes," Frederic answered. "Not good friends but they were acquainted. My own father died young. An alcoholic. My mother, my mother died I think of a broken heart. Her sister, who was going to help us come to America, disappeared in Monterey. Most everyone assumed she had died."

"By your reasoning you and Nicolas are both in danger if the murderer hates KGB agents and by extension their families."

"This is what I suspect. Someone in our company is carrying violent hatred."

Bill decided that his reasoning could be correct. The crime was violent, which could mean someone spurned in love. Nothing in the older man indicated that he would be some heartthrob killed for passion. Frederic, now, with his reputation with women would be in danger from many boyfriends and jealous husbands. *I doubt the dancer would pursue married women.* Bill thought the reverse could certainly be true. Having this conversation with the man showed him that Frederic's reputation was not just publicity but well earned. He found himself jealous of the dancer's date with Jaden. Even though Frederic's "date" seemed to be only so the man could make contact with him without raising suspicions. So this man suspected someone in the company.

Revenge was a good motive, especially because of the violent nature of the crime.

"Do you have any indication or suspicion about anyone in the company?"

Frederic pressed his muscular body back into the booth. "My belief is that someone newer to the company is the killer. Someone may have joined the company to revenge themselves on the Kurloffs."

This means that I should investigate the last people who joined the company.

Sounds logical.

When Bill did not say anything, Frederic continued. "I am trying to watch the company members to see if I notice anything that seems unusual. It is difficult because we are all upset."

"You must be careful," Bill found himself repeating for the second time today. "Now I do want you to tell me what you know about Gene Miller's disappearance."

"I have something for you." Frederic reached into his inside jacket pocket and pulled out an envelope. He silently handed it to Bill.

Bill opened the flap, which was not sealed, pulled out a piece of stationery with the California Gallery letterhead, and read, "Dear Bill, I'm sorry to have disappeared as I did, but it was necessary. Right now, your painting and I are safe. This note has been given to a man I trust completely, Frederic Melnikov. Give him your trust, too. We believe we are both in danger. Right now we are trying to protect ourselves. It is difficult for us to explain, but I assure you that you can trust Frederic. Do not look for me as this will create more danger. You and the police must be searching for me right now. If there is any way you can call off the search, please do. Thanks from your friend, Gene."

Bill's eyes narrowed as he looked over to Frederic. "You know where he is?"

"Yes."

"What is the connection between you?"

"Gene is my cousin. His mother escaped the Soviet Union and brought him to America when he was only two years old. She joined an American ballet company and kept trying to bring her sister-in-law, my mother, here. But my mother died and her sister disappeared. I wanted to go to the United States for the sake of my cousin. Most people warned me not to try."

Bill had to ask, "Your father?"

Frederick shook his head. "My father died before, of vodka. His drinking consumed him and always made me feel he did not care for me or for my mother. My aunt and Eugene retired to this small village of Pacific Grove. One day she disappeared. Gene searched for her."

Bill sank back trying to process all of the different puzzle pieces of information. Could Gene, being held somewhere, have written the letter under threat? There had been no ransom demand. Only Frederic might have the resources to pay for his cousin's life. Had someone threatened the cousins? And you would think that Gene would have mentioned or certainly bragged about his famous cousin. Bill thought of Gene's face plastered all over the papers.

Though Frederic was staring at him, the man was not saying a word. He looked so different, quite human without his stage make-up. The only thing wrong was that God-awful deep red hair. The dancer was beginning to annoy him. The man was a stranger and possibly a clever murderer. Frederic also was an astute judge of human nature and extremely observant. It irritated Bill to think that Frederic found him so transparent. Bill had never had any trouble communicating with women until he met

Jaden Steele. He realized that it was because he loved her and was afraid to do anything that might drive her away.

"What will you do?" Frederic asked quietly. "Do you trust me? I have trusted you with information about Gene that is also not common knowledge. ."

"Your relationship explains a lot. Why is this fact a secret?"

"I am, I am…I am not certain of the right words. I do not wish reporters to bother Eugene. He says he does not mind. Gene would not understand the lack of privacy when the reporters come. One time a reporter hid in my hotel room."

In spite of everything, Bill decided that he trusted him. In many interviews of criminals, he sensed when they were lying. He could be fooled, but not often. His intuition was good, like Jaden's. She trusted Frederic Melnikov. He also trusted this famous man who was also Gene Miller's cousin. "If you can communicate with Gene and assure me he is safe, I will use this letter to send a message that he has been located and is well. That should stop the newspapers and television reporters."

Frederic settled back in the booth. "Thank you. Although we did not meet until we were twenty-two, Eugene is my only living relative. If anything happened to him,

I would be devastated. He is the one who found me this property. I owe much to him. I am his partner in the art gallery."

Still surprised over this unexpected information about Frederic and Gene, Bill pulled a card from his wallet and handed it across the table. "This is my cell phone number. If you see anything, anything strange or out of the ordinary, please contact me right away. Do you own a cell phone?"

"No."

"I'll get one for you right away."

"Thank you. It's something I've thought of. Very convenient. I do not wish one of those things in my ear. People here I think are walking around talking to themselves. Then I see the black device in their ear. They walk along the beautiful cliffs without seeing the ocean."

In spite of the serious situation, Bill had to smile about people and their cell phones. He stood up and shook Frederic's hand. "Thank you for all of this information, especially the note about Gene. I was genuinely worried about him."

"And your outstanding painting is safe. He does have a buyer interested."

"Will you tell me where he is?"

"Not today. Soon," Frederic answered. "He is very frightened right now."

"Would you mind if I suggested something that might help you stay less visible, Frederic?"

"Not at all."

Bill cleared his throat, "The color of your hair is easy to spot. You could change the color to brown or something more ordinary. Just a suggestion."

"Thank you, Bill. I will consider your thought. I understand I am well known."

Jaden did not want to wear the same black silk dress she had worn to the Nutcracker, but it was her only evening dress. The dress revived the deadly memories of the opening night of the ballet. She would take it to a local thrift shop as soon as she could after the concert. Because of her disastrous affair with Sergio Panetti, she did not plan on any relationships or dates. Now, suddenly, she was going out every night. *I don't have the energy for this.* But she was looking forward to tonight.

Black looked good with her olive complexion and dark hair. It made her violet blue eyes stand out. While she was looking in the mirror, there was a knock at the door.

"Can't be Bill already."

Bobbi was standing at the door with one of her endless supply of manila folders. "Oh, I'm sorry. Sorry. You're going out."

"Yes, Bill and I are going to the symphony concert at the mission." She could not keep the excitement out of her voice. Though she loved the concert which she had seen for the first time last year, the idea of going out with Bill was more exciting than she wanted to admit. "How do I look? I don't like wearing this dress after the night at the Nutcracker, but it's my only evening outfit."

"You look great. Jaden, but if you want a different dress, I have several evening gowns. Look over this information I've printed out from the net. You'll be surprised. I'll be back in a minute with a dress that I think you'll like."

Before Jaden could answer, she disappeared into her apartment.

Jaden sat down at the kitchen table with the folder. Bobbi had searched genealogy web sites for Melnikov. The English equivalent was Miller. *This is like Smith or Jones*, she had written across the top of one paper, but she finally located Frederic's birth by searching the year. No other

Frederics, she noted. He said it was a German *name* that would not be the least bit popular in Russia. Because of that, she found the name of Frederic's father, Yuri Melnikov, and his uncle, Alexander. Both brothers died young, Yuri at forty and Alexander at age forty-five.

Her research specialist friend went to Russian name websites. A top section of the first printout was circled with a red marking pen. A translation of the common name, Melnikov, is Miller. Jaden felt her mouth drop open in surprise. She caught her breath. It was just like one of those cartoons where the light bulb pops up over one's head.

Bobbi came back with a burgundy velvet dress with a jacket. "If this fits, I think this color will look sensational. You see why I had to show this research to you?"

"Do you think it's our Gene Miller and he is related to Frederic?"

"Read the next page. Irene Melnikov and one year old son emigrated to the United States. Shortly after that Frederic's mother, Katerina, disappears from all records. Actually, both women disappear. Jaden, I've asked Edward to search for me. He has…connections, ways. With foreign records it's hard to know if they are accurate. It never hurts to find confirmation from another source."

They both knew the retired spy still had plenty of connections.

Bobbi told her, "To me it's obvious that Gene Miller and Frederic Melnikov are cousins. That's the explanation for the conversation in the park. They obviously knew each other."

Jaden would have to tell Bill.

"When is Bill coming? Do you have time to change dresses?"

"Yes. There's twenty-five minutes."

When Jaden changed, she looked into the mirror with satisfaction. Though the dress was slightly tight around the waist, the burgundy color complimented her skin.

"There. What did I tell you?" Bobbi picked up Jaden's hair brush and advanced.

"Would you let me change your hair slightly and show me your earrings."

By the time Bobbi was finished, Jaden's hair and face glowed. Instead of the dangly rhinestone earrings, she had Jaden wear a simple black pearl set that went perfectly with the dress. "This is a symphony, not a party. It's always better to be understated. Coco Chanel."

"Thank you. You have a real talent for the right clothes and make-up." She was going to say disguises but caught herself and gave Bobbi a quick hug. "You make a marvelous fairy godmother. I love it. Bobbi, how do you think the cousins became acquainted? Frederic was in Russia and Gene was here."

Bobbi nodded. "Whatever's going on, Frederic is right in the middle of it. You may think he's open. He's hiding something. How was your date? And don't go out with him again without a chaperone. Please."

"Yes, Mother. Wasn't really a date. He said he wanted to warn me about the obvious fact that there is a killer stalking the Kurloff Company. Since Igor's murder I would hardly need reminding that there was danger. When he started to talk about what a great lover he was, I prepared myself for a proposition. My ego took a hit."

"That body. All muscle. I imagine that he is quite a lover."

"Bobbi!"

"Don't pretend to be shocked. He has some reputation. And no one has ever complained. He just does not stick to one person. For me, what puts me off is that unnatural hair. I'd love to hide that horrible bottle of red hair dye."

"That was not his goal with me. When he told me I reminded him of his mother, that was deflating. He wanted to use me to talk with Bill. They met this morning. He tried to pretend we were on a date so no one would be suspicious. Bobbi, he knows something about the murder."

A soft knock at the door interrupted her next thought that he might know and not know because it might not seem important.

Bobbi went over to open the door. She caught a flicker of disappointment in Bill's dark eyes when he saw her instead of Jaden. He suddenly stared past her to Jaden.

With gleeful satisfaction Bobbi fought to control her Cheshire cat grin. Bill opened his mouth to speak but did not make a sound.

"I understand you're going to the concert at the Mission," she commented.

He nodded and smiled broadly.

Bobbi tried to remember when she had seen him look this happy. The frown lines even vanished from his forehead. There was no doubt about Bill's feelings. She wondered if everyone in the court except Jaden realized how he felt about her. She fought back a smile. He obviously did not think Jaden reminded him of his mother.

Since Bobbi knew she was now a third wheel, she said, "You two have a wonderful time. I know you will. The concert is always beautiful in the Mission chapel."

"Goodnight, Bobbi," Bill said as he helped Jaden on with her short wool coat.

"Yes, Bobbi. Thank you," Jaden offered as Roberta Petra Jones-Schmidt headed to her apartment next door.

Arizona rubbed up against Bobbi's pants leg, purring as loudly as a car engine. When the animal finally realized that the woman had no treats on her, Arizona sprang back to her perch on the post at the top of the concrete steps. If the cat was not sitting in Esther's front window, she could be counted on to be poised, sphinx-like, surveying the entire court from her perch.

They used to have vermin problems in the court. Now a mouse or a rat did not have a chance. Arizona looked peaceful and slept 90% of the day. Cats were natural hunters and the large white feline remained true to her nature.

"I'll bring you something next time," the librarian promised.

Arizona gave her one haughty glance and proceeded to lick her right front paw with her glistening pink tongue.

Jaden and Bill entered this second of the California missions founded by Father Junipero Serra. Vibrant blood red poinsettias covered the shelves on the white adobe walls, the altar, and any free spot in the long mission chapel. When the Mexican government took over California, one of its major contributions was looting and leaving the chain of Father Serra's missions in ruins. Slowly, through the years, a few people finally saw the rich historical significance of the ruined adobe buildings and worked to rebuild them. Some missions were restored, like the Carmel Mission. Others were completely replaced, like the small church in

Santa Cruz. In spite of the problems brought to California by the entry of the Spanish, the adobe brick buildings with the three foot thick whitewashed walls leave a deep impression on visitors.

Jaden often wondered about those Spanish days in old California. What would it have been like to live then? She should ask Bobbi for some reading recommendations on California history.

The symphony musicians sat crowded together in the altar area of the church, actually named San Carlos de Bonema. This mission was built on a picture perfect site by the Carmel river near the sea. Jaden had seen only the Santa Cruz Mission so she could not compare all of the sites, but this one was beautiful. Clint Eastwood's Mission ranch was next to the lovely grounds. A few blocks away stood the house that poet Robinson Jeffers built with the rocks from the shore. Hers and Bill's seats were so close to the string section in the second row that she could have reached out and touched the tips of violin bows. Had it only been a week since this orchestra played in Monterey at the nightmare performance of the Nutcracker?

All of the other performances had been cancelled, leaving a financial mess for all concerned. The dancers. The arts center.

"We're going to hear the concert in surround sound," Bill commented. *I think the music is going to be wasted on me. I'm going to have an impossible time keeping my eyes off of her. She looks more attractive than ever tonight. That deep burgundy color is beautiful on her.*

The inspiring strains of Handel's Messiah echoed from the thick adobe walls. Jaden tried to remember the story of how Handel wrote his masterpiece. She would have to ask Bobbi. Did he lock himself in a room and eventually come out with this most famous of Christmas music? *Sitting next to Bill had an effect on her memory.*

After the final standing applause died down, they stood up to leave. Bill slipped his arm over her shoulder. Even though she was trying to make the excuse to herself that the exit crowd required his keeping track of her like a child, his strong hand holding her shoulder felt like the most comfortable thing in the world. She liked that feeling.

As they walked into the cold December fog, Bill continued to hold her tightly.

"Wasn't that a beautiful performance?" she murmured as they headed for the car.

"Wonderful," Bill responded, taking a step ahead to face her. "Almost as beautiful as you." His strong arms pulled her close and he kissed her. Jaden responded to his lingering kiss. She almost forgot that they were standing in the parking lot next to his car with people brushing past them. When they finally parted, she felt unsteady.

The crowd in the parking lot was a blur.

He smiled as he clicked the Toyota's remote. Bill walked around to the passenger door to hold it open for her.

Jaden's thoughts whirled as she slid into the passenger seat.

She had not wanted him to let go.

.

"Would you like to have some coffee?" Bill asked as he pulled the car onto Rio Road heading for Highway One.

Jaden nodded, thinking that coffee was at the moment the best of her choices. Bill's kiss and her response to him made her unsure that she could keep the control that she wanted. His intentions were obvious and she could not imagine many women saying no to him.

"There's a coffee shop in the Crossroads Shopping Center that I like because it's open all night," Bill told her. "I can stop there at the end of my work shift, have coffee and a pastry and go straight home to bed."

"That would be fine," Jaden answered, trying to sound casual. "So Frederic confirmed that he and Gene were cousins."

"Yes. It's important to finally know."

Embarrassed, she stared straight into the night instead of looking at him. *Life is either a merry-go-round or a rollercoaster ride. Now I know that I was afraid of him because I like him. I can't trust myself.*

All of her promises to be careful were abandoned in the mission parking lot.

At midnight the warm *Coffee Club* was about half full. Jaden recognized one or two from the concert. Several newspapers were scattered on a small table in the entry. Bill absentmindedly picked up one while he asked the waitress, "Two, please, Nora. How are you tonight?"

Nora smiled broadly, "Bill! You look handsome tonight. You are out of uniform."

"We went to the Christmas concert at the mission. This is my friend, Jaden."

"Welcome to the Coffee Club, Jaden." The waitress looked at her with slightly narrowed, watery blue, red-rimmed eyes. Jaden must have passed inspection. The woman nodded and showed them a table for two by the window.

"Do you need a menu?" she asked.

"Would you like something to eat, Jaden? They have great pastries," Bill offered. "And coffee better than Kyle and Sydney's special secret blend. They use Green Mountain coffee from Castroville."

She shook her head. "Those pastries look good. Just coffee, though, thank you."

Nora nodded and quickly headed for the coffee station by the door to the kitchen.

"You must always pick up the paper when you come in," Jaden commented.

"Habit. I sit here and read, drink my coffee and eat a sweet roll or a bagel and try to unwind at the end of the day. Sometimes it's hard to relax, but normally the work in Carmel is quiet. The news is consistently terrible." He looked down at the paper.

"Did you see this?" He turned the headlines of the local paper so she could read aloud, 'Carmel art dealer located. He is safe and will return to work in a few days.' Sorry. I should have told all of you."

Jaden squinted to read the article without her glasses. She looked up at him. "Is he back? Why didn't you tell me?"

"I haven't actually seen him. He sent me a note through Frederic." Bill related everything that had happened during the interview except for the obvious omission of Frederic's comments about her. *Or maybe I should tell her and watch her reaction. Why is she so different from all the other women I've dated?*

The waitress returned to pour their coffee. She whispered in Bill's ear. "Nice catch. Better than that last giddy blonde."

Bill gave her a quick grin and said, "Thank you, Nora. I think so, too." He sipped his coffee and looked at Jaden across the table. She was glancing at the rest of the Herald's front page when her face visibly drained of color. She stared up at him with her lower lip trembling.

"What's wrong?" Bill asked, reaching out to her take her trembling hand.

She turned the paper around pointing to an article on the lower right hand side of the front page. He read the headline: *Homeless woman found murdered in wharf parking lot.* The first paragraph was the typical: *Police are asking for anyone who has any information about the woman or who observed suspicious activity early Wednesday morning to call in. Responses will be confidential. The woman's body was found between her shopping cart and a hedge at the side of the lot. Although police try to keep the spot free, the homeless often congregate there as it is calmer near the boat harbor and offers a little protection from the traffic on Del Monte Avenue.*

Bill questioned, "Jaden, do you think you know this woman?"

"I'm embarrassed to say that I thought she might be Bobbi checking up on me. You know how much she loves disguises. When Frederic and I got into the car I turned on the brights to scare her. I sure did. She almost dived into that hedge. When I found Bobbi at home, I was really embarrassed. Bill, I think it was the same poor, homeless woman. Most of the homeless seem to be men, so a woman stands out. If it were the same woman, she was murdered not long after we saw her."

If it were the same woman, Jaden was right. That means that it was unlikely to be a random murder. She saw Jaden with Frederic. Was that motive for murder?

"Jaden, do you think you might recognize her? Would you...," he hesitated.

She knew what he meant. "I might. I don't know. I got a good look at her in the headlights because I was trying to see if I could recognize Bobbi."

"Did Frederic seem more interested in her than what might be considered normal? Did he ask you any questions about her?"

"Yes, he did." Jaden's stomach began to churn. "He asked me why they were living there and why the government allowed it. I told him there were homeless shelters and places to get help, but sometimes the people were mentally ill for different reasons.

Drugs. Alcohol. They would not be taken away unless they committed a crime. You can't think that he would murder an old woman like that? Bill, Frederic is a famous dancer and famous personality. Why would he commit murder?"

Bill drained his coffee cup. The waitress noticed and returned to refill their mugs.

"Jaden, are you up to viewing this woman? You didn't see anything else that night? Something that might be important? We don't have to go any farther with this."

"The only way to confirm that I recognize her is to view her. There were other homeless people in the shadows that night. I don't see what good I can do for the police investigation. It seems impossible that Frederic Melnikov, a world famous dancer, would murder some homeless woman. Only if he wanted to make himself look guilty."

Or, someone else wanted to make him look guilty, Bill thought as he dialed the direct line to the Monterey police station and arranged to go to county morgue.

This is about the farthest thing from the romantic evening that I had planned.

Tonight he meant to follow Frederic's unsolicited advice and tell her how much he loved her. After that kiss in the parking lot Bill was well on the way to that moment. A shadowy murderer and circumstances were making certain that the two of them were not jelling. Now they were driving by the Castroville artichoke fields on the way to the morgue in the basement of the county hospital near Salinas.

"She's not going to look like when you saw her in the parking lot, Jaden."

"I'm guessing that dead does that to you," Jaden responded. "She'll look dead."

"O.K. I'm telling you the obvious. I'm sorry but I was worried about you. My friend in the Monterey police told me that she was stabbed. I asked them if hers and Igor's wounds could be compared. Jaden, this isn't the evening that I had planned. You are beautiful tonight. I'm…I'm sorry."
And he was.

"Not what I had in mind either. But Bill, the concert was wonderful, inspiring. Thank you for taking me. I'm sorry I read that newspaper and realized it might be the same homeless woman."

"Jaden, you are very observant. If you think she could be the same woman, we should find out for certain. Her murder could mean more than a random killing."

This is not what he had in mind either. He decided not to say it because Jaden must be aware of how he felt. Their friend, Frederic, the man with all the advice for lovers, the man both he and Jaden liked, jumped to the head of Bill's suspect list.

What would drive a famous ballet dancer to commit murder? Being famous does not make one immune from becoming a drunk, an addict, or a murderer. I ought to know that. Some killers are arrogant and believe they are smarter than anyone else. Sociopaths are like that. No conscience. You could tell them their mother died and they might not shed a tear.

"There's the hospital," Jaden said.

They parked in the back lot and found the sign that simply stated "Basement Offices" with an arrow that pointed down.

He whispered, "They don't want to frighten the patients by using *morgue*."

Jaden laughed nervously. She suddenly wished she were anywhere but here.

At the bottom of the stairs, they were met by a man in a Monterey Police uniform.

"Bill." The man greeted them and the men shook hands.

"This is Jaden Steele."

"I recognize you from the questioning after the ballet murder last week. Why do you think you know this woman?"

Jaden briefly explained the brief meeting of the homeless woman in the wharf parking lot Wednesday night. "But I saw her very clearly near the hedge."

"I wanted to see if Jaden would recognize the victim," Bill told him. "It might have something to do with the murder of the manager of the ballet company, Igor."

"Why would you think that? Well, there has been no murder in Monterey for two years and now two in one month. There could be a connection, but homeless people are easy prey. Most are mentally unstable and anything could set them off."

The disinfectant odor in the windowless, cold basement room suddenly overwhelmed Jaden. She shivered. She held her breath. Nothing could be as bad as seeing Igor Kurloff's mutilated body. A hospital gurney with what was obviously a covered body sat right in the middle of the room. *Steady. This will be over in a minute.*

Bill's strong hand gently took hold of her arm. Her heart began to pound and she held her breath. The Monterey officer slowly pulled back the blue plastic sheet.

Jaden gasped. She stared intently for about fifteen seconds, and then nodded. "I'm about ninety-five percent certain that was the woman I saw in the wharf parking lot. Why would anyone kill her?"

"I have no idea, Mrs. Steele," the officer replied. "Except that there's some really crazy people in this world. I was hoping that you had seen something that might give us a clue. When you said you had seen a homeless woman there, I was almost positive it was her. According to the street men we interviewed, there were no other homeless women in the area."

Jaden felt grateful when he covered the woman's head with the sheet again. "The only thing odd about her is her feet. They're misshapen. Maybe some kind of arthritis or an accident."

Jaden swallowed hard. "Why?" was all she could force out in a choked whisper. Her mind raced back to how Frederic was startled by the woman. And she was a handicapped person, with those feet.

"Would you send me a copy of the forensic report?" Bill asked.

"Be glad to." He shook his head. "Two murders in one week. If nothing else, it is an enormous coincidence."

At three a.m. Jaden forced herself to pull her clothes off before she slipped into bed. *I can't ruin Bobbi's beautiful dress.* If they had been her own clothes they would have gone to bed with her. She did not even search for her pajamas, crawling under the covers in her bra and panties thinking that she would change after a short nap. Bill must have been exhausted, too. He made no move to kiss her again before or after she opened her door. Her tired, swollen eyes refused to stay open. Before Jaden fell into a deep sleep she thought of him with a mixture of relief and regret. That kiss in the parking lot was enough for one night. It awakened too many feelings in her that she wanted to keep buried. *Be careful, Jaden.*

More alarming, Jaden woke in a drowsy haze with his face swirling in front of her. Not just his face alone. Frederic's face, looking unreal in his stage makeup, melted into the swirl along with the white face of the dead woman and Igor's bloodied face pressed up against the bedroom window.

Jaden woke with a muffled shriek. Her heart was thudding and she was shaking.

It took her several seconds to realize that she was safe in her own apartment. Igor's face was fading, but had she seen two faces? Maybe one a shadow with no features. *Just a nightmare.* A long, deep sigh of relief escaped her lips. Her heart slowly returned to its normal pace.

Her head was pounding. She would take some aspirin. *I should eat something first and drink plenty of water with the pills.* Before she could do anything, the phone rang. The noise intensified the pounding in her head.

Jaden forced herself to pick up the receiver. "Hello."

"Jaden?" It took a few seconds to identify the familiar voice.

"Yes."

"Good morning. It's McKenzie. Do you have a cold? You sound stuffy."

"McKenzie. No, just exhausted. How are you?" *Attorney McKenzie Anderson represented Bobbi in her sensational murder trial and represented Jaden when the police suspected her of murdering her lover, Sergio Panetti.* She liked the handsome lawyer. He was easy to talk to.

"Fine. I'm sorry. Did I wake you?"

"No. No, McKenzie. We went to a concert at the Carmel Mission last night but I didn't get in until three a.m." *She should not have said that.* Jaden did not want to go through the whole story about last night with him now.

"Who is keeping you up until three in the morning? I thought you would be awake because of opening the store."

Jaden looked at the clock. *Eight-thirty!* She rarely slept in after seven.

"I'm glad you called. I have to get down there in less than an hour so I can open up by ten. Hal's coming in but not until this afternoon. It's good to hear your voice. How is San Diego?"

"San Diego is great, but I'm here at my condo in Monterey. Are you free for lunch? I'd love to see you. I've missed you."

"That would be wonderful, McKenzie." And a good way to keep her mind off Bill. McKenzie was fun and even tempered.

"How about *The Mad Hatters* since it is right next to your store?"

"Great!" She appreciated staying in the court to be near the shop.

"I'll be over at twelve-thirty."

After he hung up, Jaden made coffee and toast. Her stomach felt queasy, which was to be expected after spending some of the morning at the county morgue in the basement of the hospital. Handy if you lose a patient, she thought cynically.

Jaden had committed every detail of their visit to see the homeless woman to memory. She already sensed that the murders were connected. Why kill her? What could she possibly have done to deserve that fate in life? To be homeless, friendless, and then killed. The woman's misshapen feet were important. Jaden already thought that she knew why. Could that pitiful creature possibly ever have been one of those graceful ballerinas? Some dancer's feet could get grotesque.

She felt better after her shower and chose a white silk long sleeved blouse to wear with her black wool pants. Jaden studied the scars on her arms, remembering the moment Marian Panetti tried to shoot her and shattered the display case instead, sending shards rifling everywhere. The scars barely showed, but Jaden had thrown away anything sleeveless. The marks faded but would always be a reminder of how stupid she had been with that worthless man. One romantic week-end turned into a nightmare. Being vulnerable was no excuse for plain stupidity. She did not seem to be able to let go of the anger at herself for believing Sergio's well practiced lies.

Jaden answered a soft knock at the door.

"Bobbi, come in."

The librarian entered carrying one of what must be her hundred manila folders.

"How about coffee?" Jaden offered.

"Great, you make the best," Bobbi placed the folder on the kitchen table. "I'd like coffee and can't wait to hear what went on last night, if you want to tell me."

"Bobbi, I…you are never going to believe what happened." She began with their visit to the coffee shop and went on with the story from there.

Normally Bobbi could keep a straight face, but there was no hiding the confused expression in her golden-flecked eyes. When she was thoughtful, her eyes appeared to slant more than ever.

"She was killed by a single knife wound to the chest. The killer caught her from behind and probably was left handed. Bobbi, she had calloused feet and toes. I remember hearing about the foot problems dancers have. Kyle said many ballerinas have horrible feet because of dancing on their toes." Jaden took another welcome sip of her coffee. "Modern dancers go barefoot. They can develop callouses, but nothing like what I saw."

Bobbi offered, "That's right. Lots of trivia is packed into a librarian's head."

"Bill was going to ask Nicolas to look at pictures of the dead woman's feet. If she were a ballerina at some point in time, this means she could have recognized someone or they recognized her. She was seen as a danger to them."

"Someone knew her? It's beyond coincidence, but not impossible."

"Bobbi, there are very few homeless women in the area. Last year she was arrested for breaking into and living in vacation homes. A homeless woman who was also a ballerina who was also murdered makes me uneasy. And there's something I feel uneasy about, something I should remember. Do you ever feel that way?"

"Jaden, more than uneasy. I'm absent-minded, too, and write down everything on my calendar. You have great instincts. I feel what you sense. The killer is here, nearby. The person saw you with Frederic. Be very careful. Or it could also be that our charming ballet star snapped for some reason none of us understand."

"I just don't believe he could do it. Why? He has everything."

"Some people have all the money in the world and they embezzle more, they do drugs, abuse others. Jaden, I'll never understand people. I'm going to do some more research on the families like the Kurloff's. It is not easy because of the record keeping in the old Soviet Union. I'll ask for some help from Edward. Of course he has the best information connections on the planet. He's also a marvelous analyst. That was his job until he retired last year. He said he liked field work a lot more."

"He got those genes honestly from his mother. I've told Esther that whatever is tucked inside her head would make a sensational book, but, unlike some, she is true to the oath of keeping whatever she knows a secret."

A quick smile sparkled in Bobbi's golden, almond shaped eyes. "To change the conversation, tell me I was right about McKenzie Anderson."

The abrupt change in subject caught Jaden by surprise. While the early part of Esther's life might be a secret, nothing else stayed out of the Dolores Court news chain.

Jaden stared at the steam rising out of her coffee cup. "You're annoying."

"I know he's here. He wants you to go out with him, doesn't he?"

"Yes, we have a date for lunch, and I'm certain he wants to go out again."

Bobbi went to the sink with her cup. She rinsed it out and put it in the dish rack. "Bill won't be happy."

"Too bad. I don't know if it's possible for Bill to be happy. He's so moody. At least McKenzie is even tempered and lots of fun."

Bobbi's response was a slight chuckle.

Jaden frowned. Bobbi was way too observant when it was none of her business.

On the way out of the apartment, Jaden could not help comparing the two men. McKenzie was charming. Why did she wish that she had another date with Bill?

As she walked to the stairs, she noticed that Arizona's perch was empty. She glanced in Esther's window to see the huge white cat sleeping in the windowsill. Cats must sleep twenty plus hours a day.

Arizona must sleep with one eye open. Anyone who walked downstairs had a cat partner. This morning Jaden did not have company walking down the concrete steps.

"My, don't we look elegant today," Kyle Foster commented as he was setting the Mad Hatter's outdoor tables.

"Thank you, Kyle."

The tall man stopped working to stare at her. "A bit pale, aren't we? Big night? Our Cinderella decided to go to the ball."

"Not what you're thinking. I'll tell you and Sydney later."

"Promise."

Short, heavyset Sydney came out of the café door. "Kyle, the strawberries are going bad. Let's send Enrique to the store when he comes. Good morning, Jaden. How was the concert?" His hazel eyes narrowed. "Stayed up late, did we?"

"Is it that obvious?"

"Maybe just a touch of make-up needed today. I want to hear all about the symphony. Let me get you some hot coffee with real cream. It will do wonders for you," Sydney offered.

"And maybe more than a touch of make-up," Kyle advised.

"Should I wear a mask? I'll run upstairs before lunch and try to do something. Secret keeping is difficult around here. McKenzie Anderson is coming to lunch."

"The lawyer?" Sydney returned with a giant mug of coffee for her. "He's back?"

"Can you get us an invitation to his condo sometime? We hear he has a view of the whole bay." Kyle asked, "I imagine *you've* already had an invite. McKenzie likes you."

"Stop being so catty," Jaden said, turning to go to the door of the shop. "Work time. Thank you for the coffee, Sydney. That real cream was wonderful. Can't do that all the time, though."

Of course the first thing that Jaden did was to peer into the store's bathroom mirror. A pale faced stranger stared back at her. The ghostly reflection grinned weakly.

All she could hope was that some of her color would return during the morning.

There was make-up, as Kyle and Sydney had already advised.

She thought of the end of her conversation with Bobbi. "Jaden, there's a real connection in the murders. I feel it in my bones. And I'm pretty jealous because McKenzie only called me to say hello. You have two men after you."

"They are not *after me.*"

"You can't be that dense, Jaden. I'll be in my apartment if you need protection."

"Bobbi," she protested as her friend left.

The morning was semi-busy and she never found time to check the internet orders. Usually she looked at the store's website before opening and promptly arranged to wrap anything ordered by mail the same day. They were known for their service. She would have to stay after the store closed to fill any orders.

When the bell on the door jangled about twelve-fifteen, McKenzie's tall figure entered the store just as the telephone rang.

"A Slice of Carmel," she answered.

"Jaden Steele?" She recognized the soft accented voice immediately.

"Frederic. How are you?" *Are you a clever murderer?* She burned to ask.

"I am well, thank you. The officer, Bill, is here. He brought me a small phone. We put in both of your numbers, his, and the Carmel police in the phone so I have only to press one button. This is amazing. I have been meaning to buy this. "

Jaden knew that Bill must have questioned Frederic again. He may have tried to disguise the fact that he was interviewing by small talk. And, calls from that phone could be traced because of the billing. It occurred to her that Frederic might need a lawyer and here was one successful defense attorney right in front of her.

"Thank you, Jaden Steele. I will press the end button as Bill tells me."

"Goodbye, Frederic." She hung up the phone and smiled at McKenzie.

"Jaden, you look wonderful." He came over to hug her and kissed her forehead.

You are the first person today to tell me that. My face must have some color now. Good, because she never had a chance for that touch of magic make-up that the chefs certainly recommended as a recipe du jour.

"Why didn't you tell us you were coming?" she asked.

"I just decided yesterday. When I saw the story of Igor Kurloff's murder, I thought of you all here and called Bobbi. She told me what happened and that the identity of the killer was still a mystery. Her story has been nagging at me so I had my secretary rearrange my schedule for a week. I've been meaning to come up to see the condo and you anyway. It's obvious you two can't avoid a mystery."

"Bobbi would love to see you." Ignoring his last remark, Jaden drew her keys out of her pocket.

"I'd like to see her, too, but I wanted to talk to you first." He moved close to her when he reached out for the door handle to open it again.

For some reason his nearness made her think of her husband, Brent. The two had similar personalities. Jaden turned the paper clock hands to one-thirty and they stepped out the door into the bright winter sunlight. Because she did not want customers wandering into the store, she locked the door even though they would be nearby in the court. Better to be cautious.

"Hal will be here soon," Jaden said.

McKenzie pulled out a chair at the table for her to sit and took the chair next to her, not across the table. It made more sense as the tables were large.

"Thank you, McKenzie." She looked into his clear blue eyes.

His response was a grin that always made her think of how boyish, innocent, and easy to underestimate he must look in court. Just like Esther Stennis, those clear blue eyes missed nothing.

Arizona trotted down the stairs when she saw Jaden and brushed up against her legs. "That white fur must be all over my slacks, Arizona." She tried to push the cat away, which made the animal even more determined and demanding.

"Isn't that the cat Kyle and Sydney brought back from Arizona?" McKenzie asked. "They took their relief truck to the flooding by the Colorado River last year."

A familiar voice said, "Jaden, I'm sorry. Let me take her up to my apartment."

Jaden had been thinking of Esther.

McKenzie stood up to hug the eighty-seven year old woman. "McKenzie. So good to see you again. Will you be staying long?"

"A week. Won't you join us?" he asked.

"Oh, no, thank you. I was just going on my walk. But I will take this cat away from Jaden's black wool slacks." She picked up the animal, which snuggled into her arms without protest. "Will you be staying in Carmel for a while?"

"Yes. I've come up to see Jaden, I mean, Jaden and everyone. And I was thinking of having a housewarming party at my condo. I'll invite everyone who lives in the court."

"That would be wonderful," Esther answered. "So good to see you and I will take Arizona up to my apartment now. Have a nice lunch." She turned to go up the stairs.

"She's amazing," McKenzie said as he sat down again.

Enrique appeared with two menus. "Mr. Anderson. How are you?"

"Fine. How is your family, Enrique?"

"They are doing well. My son is now two years old. Big boy."

"Do you still have the grilled tuna salad?" McKenzie asked.

Enrique nodded.

"That's my favorite, too," Jaden said.

"Then let's have that, Enrique. Jaden, what would you like to drink?"

"Coffee, thank you."

"Iced raspberry tea, Enrique." McKenzie handed the menus back.

Enrique disappeared into the front door of the small restaurant.

"Jaden, I've been thinking about you a lot," McKenzie began. "How have you been? That time Marian Panetti almost killed you has been running through my mind all year. I would never want anything to happen to you. Jaden, I…."

Kyle interrupted his speech by bringing a mug, a small pot of hot coffee, and the tall glass of iced tea on a tray. "Hello, McKenzie. Welcome back to Carmel."

The lawyer stood up and shook hands with Kyle. "Thank you. Good to be here."

"How long are you planning to stay?"

"Not sure. Love a month here. I really need a vacation." McKenzie sat down again.

"Wonderful. We hope to see you a lot. Those salads will be right up."

"Where was I? Jaden, I missed you." He poured steaming coffee into her mug.

"Thank you, McKenzie. I missed you, too. Of course all of us missed you. I can't thank you enough for helping me when Sergio was killed and I know Bobbi will be forever grateful about how much you helped her through that horrible trial." She was not certain about mentioning Frederic. In the first place he was at the top of the suspect list. If she were certain he was innocent she would ask McKenzie about representing the dancer. In our justice system, though, everyone was entitled to legal representation, and they did not get any better than McKenzie Anderson.

Although the weather was cool, McKenzie took a huge gulp of his iced tea.

"Jaden, it's so good to see you. I'd love to take you out to dinner tonight. I've asked Bobbi to join us just for a few minutes now. Her schedule is 1-8 p.m. today."

My social life is a whirl. She could not help the quick smile that crossed her face. Bobbi was absolutely correct. She should enjoy this popularity.

"Do you have plans for dinner?"

"No, McKenzie. I am tired and don't know if I would be a good companion tonight." Her big plans included going to bed early.

"We won't stay out late. Just dinner. You have to eat anyway." He gave her that irresistible little boy look.

"Thank you, McKenzie, if you don't mind a short evening. I am tired and of course have to work tomorrow."

"I understand," he gently put his hand on hers. "I promise you we will have a wonderful dinner and come right back to Dolores Court."

Out of the corner of her eye, she saw Kyle smiling knowingly at them. The latest Dolores Court news flash was already in viral publication.

Hal, the former owner of the cutlery store, was coming in to work. "McKenzie!" He came over to shake the lawyer's hand. "How long have you been in town? Will you stay for a while?"

"Just arrived. I'm not certain about the time I can stay here."

"Sandy and I want to have you over for dinner. And Jaden, too."

"I want to congratulate you on your marriage, Hal. You and Sandy deserve to be happy together."

"Thanks. It's a wonderful life. Both of us were nervous about it. Both widowed and hesitant to start new relationships. I can recommend it to anyone, though." He smiled at Jaden.

She could have thrown her cup at him.

"Why don't you two stay out for a while. I'll open the store."

"That's not necessary, Hal."

"Yes, it is. You need to relax."

He did not say that she looked tired.

Since Jaden closed the store at five that ought to leave her some time to take a quick nap. She did not need to change clothes. She would add a coat and some jewelry. One of Bobbi's makeup sessions would be a God-send today.

Her quick glances in the mirror all day never showed any improvement. Maybe she should have put McKenzie off for a while. She felt tired enough to want a week's vacation. He was right, though. She did have to eat.

Bill Amirkhanian spent an hour going over the forensic report of the homeless woman's autopsy. She died of a knife wound. If she had not died of that, cirrhosis of the liver would have caught her in probably less than twelve months.. In spite of being heavyset, she was malnourished. As for anything else, she had misshapen feet, probably from wearing castoff shoes. He decided to bring the information to Jaden as soon as possible. And Bill thought of Edward with all of his connections. Maybe there was some way he could help with identification. Something was nagging him.

It was a beautiful, bright day, so for his lunch, Bill walked back from the police station at Junipero and Fourth to Dolores court. He could get something at home, or, if Jaden had not eaten yet, he would invite her to have lunch at The Mad Hatter's. Jaden was beautiful last night in spite of the nightmarish end of the evening. He smiled to himself at the thought of seeing her again.

As he walked by the display window of A Slice of Carmel into the inviting court, he saw Jaden right away, sitting with that lawyer, McKenzie Anderson. They were deep in conversation and she was smiling at him. A wave of jealousy surged through him. He did not want to talk to her with that man there and would have dashed past them up the stairs to his apartment if Kyle, holding two plates with salad, had not almost bumped into him. "Bill! Hello." Jaden and McKenzie both turned.

Kyle set the plates on their table. "Bill, would you like some lunch or coffee?"

He answered by shaking his head. He needed to dash up the stairs to escape.

"Were you going upstairs?" Jaden asked.

No, I was coming to see you, not you with that damned lawyer. He wanted to growl and get away as soon as possible.

"Can you join us?" Jaden asked. "McKenzie's just flown up from San Diego. He called me this morning."

McKenzie forced a smile. "Actually, I drove. It's a way for me to relax."

You always look too relaxed. Bill realized he was clenching his teeth. *And she was the first person you called, naturally.* Bill prayed that his head would clear.

Jaden persisted, "I was just going to tell McKenzie what happened last night. Do you have the autopsy report yet?"

McKenzie offered, "Please join us."

When Jaden began the story of the events of the night before, McKenzie slowly realized what he already suspected about Bill. He really likes her, too. McKenzie thought he should not have left Jaden for so many months, but his law practice was in San Diego.

He could start a second office in Carmel or Monterey. *It's only an hour and a half flight.* Since Bobbi's famous trial he had more clients than he could handle, and certainly could use an associate. He only hesitated because, although there were plenty of attorneys looking for employment, he only wanted to work with the best.

Obviously interested, Kyle lingered at the table.

"I will have coffee, Kyle. Jaden and I did not get back until three and I can't seem to wake up today." Bill enjoyed the look on McKenzie's face. When he found out they spent the early morning in the morgue, his envious look would vanish. What has the man got except good looks, success, and a pleasant personality?

A slight sigh that he hoped no one heard escaped through his clenched teeth.

Kyle went back to the kitchen for the coffee and an order at another table.

"There's nothing unusual about the report. One knife wound in the chest killed her. There was no slashing, like the way Igor Kurloff was killed. She was malnourished with an enlarged liver. If she kept that up, she probably would not have lived more than a year or so. She needed to see a podiatrist. She had big callouses on her feet and toes. They must have hurt. Maybe she was a soccer player."

Kyle was setting another pot of coffee down. "Maybe she was a ballerina."

They all turned to look up at him.

Bill asked with a whisper, "Why did you say that, Kyle?"

"En pointe," Jaden commented.

Kyle said, "You know that I love the graceful dance form of ballet. Those women who dance on their toes can be torture victims. There's a group of people who would like to outlaw torture, but they never mention those graceful ballerinas. In order to dance on their toes, over the years they form huge callouses and can have endless foot trouble."

Bill felt as though a bolt of lightning had struck him. "We need to show pictures of her feet to one of the dance company. And pictures of her." He added, exchanging a look with Jaden.

He stood up. If that old woman had been a dancer, the killing was not just the random murder of a homeless derelict. And the only person connected with the case, the one who saw her in the parking lot and seemed surprised to see her, was Frederic Melnikov. It would have been very difficult for her to see Frederic. As impossible as it seemed, he was the chief suspect. So far there was a lot of circumstantial evidence. It really would not take much more to make an arrest of one of the world's most famous ballet stars.

"There does not seem to be any way to identify the poor woman. I almost can guarantee you that the murderer knew her. I feel it." Jaden gulped her coffee.

She felt that she was reading Bill's mind while he was dashing up the steps. He was going to have someone confirm what Kyle had said about ballerina's feet.

If the dead woman were a ballet dancer that was too much of a coincidence. Someone in the Kurloff Company knew her. They recognized the poor old derelict and killed her, or, the reverse could be true. She recognized someone and because of that she had to die.

"How could anyone from a Russian ballet company know a homeless woman living on the streets in Monterey?" was McKenzie's logical question.

"Someone knew her. There have been very few homeless women in our area in the last year, not since that Sarah was jailed for breaking into vacation homes. To find a homeless woman who was also a ballerina makes me uneasy."

Bobbi came down the stairs.

"Uneasy is a mild reaction. You have good instincts and I feel the same way you do. There's a killer here and whoever it is has seen you with Frederic. Be careful."

Jaden's hand automatically slipped into the pocket of her slacks and touched the handle of her Monarch knife. For a time she left it in her apartment but now wherever she went, her pet Monarch was going with her.

Bobbi noticed her reaction and understood. "I'm going to research those families like the Kurloff's more, to see what I can find. And I'll ask for some help from Edward. He's got super information connections. Edward is a great analyst."

"And Esther. I've told Esther that all of those facts tucked into her head would make a great book. Unlike some, though, she is true to the oath of keeping secrets."

When McKenzie went into the Mad Hatters to pay the bill, a quick smile lit Bobbi's golden, almond shaped eyes. "Tell me I was right about McKenzie Anderson." Her abrupt change of subject caught Jaden by surprise. While Esther's life may always be a secret, nothing stayed out of the Dolores Court news chain.

She kept her eyes riveted on her cooling tea. "You are so sharp it's annoying, Bobbi."

"He wants you to go out with him, doesn't he?"

"Yes, we have a date tonight."

Bobbi rose and said, "Work Time." She lowered her voice, "Bill won't be happy."

"That's too bad. I've rarely seen him happy. He's moody. At least McKenzie is even tempered and lots of fun."

Bobbi's answer was a slight chuckle, which could have meant anything.

On the way back to the store, Jaden could not help comparing the two men. McKenzie was charming. Why did she wish that tonight she had another date with Bill?

When they closed the store, Hal commented, "Did you notice someone's been putting dog treats in that container in front of Gene's gallery. Have you heard when he's coming back?"

"No. I thought he would be back by now. He was always so good about opening the gallery and now it's been closed for a week. Could I be nosy? Has he paid his lease for next year?"

"Yes, but I'm not certain if Gene really pays it. The payment is made from Switzerland. I'd better not talk about it anymore, Jaden. I know you would not want me to be telling people how you pay your lease, but Gene's sudden disappearance was so strange."

"I'm sorry, Hal. My curiosity makes me too nosy sometimes."

"Sandy does want to have you and Bill over for dinner. Now I've invited McKenzie. Maybe we could have you over twice."

"Bill works some nights, so it will be harder to pin him down."

Hal looked at her. "I thought you were going out with him again tonight."

"No. I have a date with McKenzie."

The former owner's laugh filled the store. "And here I was giving you advice."

Jaden felt herself blushing. "Bill and McKenzie both have their good points. I'm not ready for a serious relationship, Hal."

"And that dancer likes you, too."

Jaden started to say because *I remind him of his mother.*

Jaden pulled her black silk dress and wool jacket from the closet. McKenzie would not recognize the dress. Her half hour nap had revived her. As soon as she lay on the bed her body surrendered to a deep sleep. Her dreams were peppered with jigsaw puzzles flying everywhere around her. They flew at her, moaning like nightmare haunts. She ran to escape the wild pieces that were angry because she could not assemble them into a picture.

The identity of the killer was not just eluding her, but also Bobbi, Bill, and the Monterey Police. If she had enough time after she got ready, Jaden would start making notes about what happened from the moment the ballet troop had crowded into the door of her shop. That might help her notice something that did not seem important at the time, or a pattern.

She fastened the clasp of a necklace with onyx beads and a cameo that had belonged to her grandmother. Jaden always thought that it looked perfect with her dress.

Maybe she would keep it after all. Her earrings were more modern onyx but looked like they matched the necklace. The outfit was dramatic in spite of its simplicity.

Since McKenzie was not coming for another half hour she sat down with some three by five cards and started to write. She wrote down the names of the people in the company who came into the store. She might have forgotten some. And then there were locals in the production. What happened so far could indicate a killer who knew the area. She spoke to herself,

"I'll ask Edward and Esther for help."

"Stolen knife" received a card all its own. Who could have stolen the knife and hidden it in front of the whole company? The visitors from the company mostly wore slacks and t-shirts. After they left Carmel they toured down the coast to Big Sur. Would someone have been able to conceal a knife for that long? A woman. A woman could hide the knife easier than a man. Women carried purses and floppier jackets with pockets.

Would a woman have the strength to kill a big man like Igor? Most people would assume not. Jaden knew that she herself had the knowledge and training to do it.

Jaden was trying the concentration system her grandfather had taught her to use before knife throwing. Deep breaths.

Clear your mind.

The ring of the phone interrupted her attempt. She answered with an absent minded "Hello."

Bill's voice echoed into her ears. "Jaden. How are you? We had such a long night that I've been worried about you."

This really did not seem typical of Bill. They did have a long night and morning.

"Bill, were you able to find out anything from Nicolas Kurloff?"

"Yes. I can come over this evening and tell you what we know so far. We talked with him this afternoon at the hotel. Later I showed the director of the Monterey Dance Academy pictures of the dead woman's feet. He thought she was a ballerina with damage from toe dancing."

"Oh, I'm sorry, Bill. I'm going out to dinner in a few minutes."

There was a silence before he said, "I'm sorry, too. Goodnight, Jaden."

The line droned in her ear. *How rude. He hung up before I could say goodbye.* "I'm glad that I'm going out with McKenzie," Jaden told herself, although she recognized that Bill had guessed the identity of her date and did not like her plans.

It's none of his business anyway.

She picked up the cards in one angry swoop and put them into her desk drawer.

None of his business. Jaden thought about Bill last night. The way that he kissed her left no doubt in her mind that Bobbi was right all along. Usually Jaden was a lot more aware of her feelings. Sergio made a fool out of her. She could not blame him forever, though, for what was her mistake. *Blaming someone else is too easy.* The buck stops here, not there.

I'd better keep my relationships on an even course and be careful.

A knock at the door made her speculations vanish. *It's a good thing that I'm going out with McKenzie to keep my mind off of all of this.*

McKenzie was standing at her entryway, staring admiringly. "You look sensational."

"Thank you, McKenzie." She picked up her evening bag containing her cell phone and her Monarch knife. She took Bobbi's warning seriously. From now on the knife would always be in her pocket or her purse.

He helped her with her jacket.

As Jaden and McKenzie were starting down the first step of the stairs, Arizona bolted down with her usual lightning bolt burst of speed.

"Danger. Cat," McKenzie commented.

The cat waited at the bottom of the stairs as proud and haughty as normal. Jaden reached down to pet her. Satisfied, the white ball of fluff ambled up the steps.

Once in the car Jaden settled down in the comfortable beige leather seat. She felt comfortable with McKenzie.

The lawyer said, "Jaden, you look great. Life in Carmel must agree with you."

"It does, McKenzie. I feel as though I've lived here longer than sixteen months. It's like I've known some of my neighbors all of my life."

"That's interesting." McKenzie turned from Carpenter Street onto the freeway. In about a mile he took the Munras exit to downtown Monterey.

"Where are we going?" Jaden asked.

"I have a favorite restaurant next to the wharf. Whenever I have the time, this is where I go for a special dinner. I think you'll like it."

Brilliant strings of white icicle lights on the roofs decorated a wine tasting room, the restaurant called the "Sea Shadows."

Since it was the middle of the week in December, Jaden was surprised to find the restaurant almost completely full. The hostess smiled broadly when she saw them.

"Mr. Anderson, welcome. So good to see you. It's been a while. "

Jaden wondered if the woman had a remarkable memory for names or just for McKenzie. There were people who could remember names. She was pretty good herself. They were seated at a separate table that McKenzie had reserved by the fire.

Jaden ordered one of the evening specials, a teriyaki chicken.

McKenzie ordered a bottle of Brassfield sauvignon blanc at Jaden's suggestion. After he sampled the wine, McKenzie nodded toward Jaden, "Very good."

With the wine and the warm fire and the view of the decorated lights on the boats with the background of Fisherman's Wharf, Jaden finally relaxed back into her chair.

Jaden would have eaten their first course, a Boston clam chowder, in two minutes if it had not been so hot.

"This is even better than Sydney's." She took another sip of the creamy delight.

"Wait for the rest," McKenzie said, smiling at her with his clear eyes sparkling.

The waiter lifted the cover of their steaming plates. Jaden breathed in a heavenly scent of oriental spices and chicken. Her first bite of the chicken made her want to demolish the dish. She did not want to embarrass McKenzie.

Why was she so hungry?

An oriental fried rice and perfectly steamed broccoli completed the meal.

Normally she would take something home for a meal the next day.

Not tonight. She ate every grain of rice.

"Didn't like it?" Mackenzie said with a chuckle as he stared at her empty plate.

"That was delicious. I've never been here. Obviously many other people know about it."

"I found it one day when I did not want to deal with the tourist crowds on the wharf. It has the same beautiful view of the boats in the harbor."

The yachts sparkled with Christmas lights in honor of the season. Some were varicolored, some solid white, blue, or green. All of the lights cast rippled light show reflections in the dark water of the boat harbor.

After coffee, McKenzie suggested, "Let's walk around a little before we go home. Outside the lights are so vivid."

They walked quietly together to the calm water's edge.

"It is beautiful." At first Jaden did not see any of the homeless people who lived in the shadows. Many were as timid as feral cats that waited for people to leave before they sneaked out. The slightest move toward them and they would streak into the shadows of their private world.

In response McKenzie took her hand and led her to a bench by the sidewalk in front of the harbor. "Would you like to sit for a few minutes to watch the bay?"

"All right," Jaden answered, knowing that McKenzie did not have the view in mind. This bright, clear night with thousands of Christmas lights on the boats was a perfect moment to sit, relax, and give way to the romantic scene.

As soon as they sat down on the cold bench, a sound nearby made her turn. An old, gray-haired man in a frayed dark sport coat was rummaging through a sidewalk trash container. He must not have heard about the killing. Why should he know? The homeless did not have cell phones, only word of mouth information. Many were alcoholics who did not often carry on intelligent conversations. Many could not even remember conversations from a day or an hour earlier.

McKenzie slipped his arm over her shoulder. "San Diego is beautiful in a different way. There's a long river walk."

"I've never been to San Diego," Jaden answered slowly, staring intently at the clear horizon and the sparkling lights of Santa Cruz at the north end of the bay. "Once Brent and I went to Disneyland, but that is not really seeing California, is it?"

"Your husband?"

Jaden swallowed hard. The hot tears that she felt welling in her eyes made her realize that she was still in mourning. Would that empty hollow ever go away? Just when she thought those feelings were buried, they erupted uncontrollably to the surface.

She nodded, unable to speak.

McKenzie spoke gently. "I'd be glad to show you the San Diego area. Would you like to come down sometime? The flight is only an hour and a half."

"I have the shop to run, McKenzie. The work time I contracted with Hal is almost over. Then the shop will be my responsibility."

"Can you hire someone part time?"

"The rest of the winter will be quieter and I know I can handle the work. I'll have to wait until June to see if I can afford help. It's not just the salary, but the taxes and insurance. Being an employer can be a total headache. And I think it's getting worse."

McKenzie thought about his successful practice. They turned clients away every week. He started out with a good practice. The Petra-Jones trial shot him out of a cannon into a blanket of fame. He had only taken her case because he knew the indictment to be unfair and politically motivated. All of the evidence proved Roberta's innocence. When the attractive woman sat in his office he knew she was innocent. It was not those golden brown, cat-like eyes. Actually those made her look seductive and contributed to the femme fatale image made up by the tabloids. He finally convinced her to wear her glasses all the time. The first time she came to court he had to smile. She transformed herself to look all business in her gray suit and glasses.

He could offer to help Jaden. No, that was not the way to her heart. She was trying her best to make it on her own.

With his free hand he touched her chin and turned her face to his. She leaned toward him, willing, but her favorite John Denver song echoed from her handbag.

"Take me home, country road…"

"Oh, a call," She reached down to open the bag and pull out her cell phone.

Sighing deeply, McKenzie slowly pulled his hands back.

"Hello."

For a few seconds Jaden heard nothing. "Can't be a solicitor," she muttered, about ready to end the call with her poised forefinger. Suddenly a familiar, accented voice that seemed far away broke the uneasy silence on the line..

"Jaden...Steele."

Though the words were barely audible, she recognized the voice.

"Frederic?"

"I...have…called…to Bill for help. And...911. I…call…you now."

"Frederic, where are you? What is wrong?" Her stomach knotted.

"Tried to…kill…us." The voice seemed farther away, fading as she listened.

Bile rose in her throat, "Frederic, can you say any more? Where are you?"

"Hotel…Exercise room…I…."

Suddenly she heard a clunk. Though Frederic was silent, Jaden knew from some muffled static that the phone was still in operation. She jumped up. Frederic had not ended the call deliberately.

The lights on the harbor, the warm dinner, and everything else vanished until she shook her head. That brought reality crashing down on her.

"McKenzie! Let's get to the hotel! Running will be faster than trying to park the car!"

She jumped up and began to run across the wharf parking lot to Del Monte Avenue. As soon as there was a break in the traffic she dashed across the street, leaving McKenzie trapped on the beach side by a sudden rush of traffic.

Her heart was thundering uncontrollably as she dashed between the people on the sidewalk. McKenzie finally caught up with her at the first corner, Franklin Street.

"Jaden, what's happened?"

"Frederic! He's in trouble! He said, 'He tried to kill us.' We should have known! We should have known! McKenzie, we have to get to the hotel right now! Something's happened there."

"How could you know? How could you read some killer's mind?"

"Because if Frederic were not the killer, he is in danger. We were looking at things the wrong way!"

McKenzie suddenly yanked her arm and pulled her back to him.

"Jaden!"

She had almost stepped off the curb in front of the traffic. Car horns suddenly blared in her ears. They had to wait eternal seconds to cross the busy street. Once the signal changed they ran the block and a half to the hotel.

In the Monterey Hotel lobby guests were gathered in groups, talking and also peering out the large picture window to the street. Blaring sirens filled the air.

"Frederic said he called 911. McKenzie, the stairs are in the corner." She felt her throat tighten in a silent scream.

Not Frederic. Not Frederic.

Jaden frantically ran up to the second floor, searching for the exercise room. Dance company members were scrambling out of their rooms, tying on robes or dressed in pajamas and nightgown. Some were murmuring, "Is it a fire? A fire?"

Jaden caught one man's arm, "Where is the exercise room?"

He pointed to the end of the hall.

The last door read, "Spa and exercise room. Guests only. Your room key opens the door." Jaden heard the bubbling noise of a hot tub.

But they did not need a room key. The door was open a few inches. McKenzie pushed it open all the way. Jaden gasped.

A commanding voice behind them ordered, "Get some of those towels!"

Open mouthed, Jaden realized that the voice belonged to Edward Stennis. Edward was dressed as the homeless man she had seen in the parking lot by the restaurant. He followed us here! He's been following me all night. If only he had followed Frederic!

Wearing only wet swim trunks, Frederic was sitting up but curled almost in a fetal position next to the hot tub door. Blood covered his bare arms and legs, and the floor. Jaden realized that he was trying to stop the bleeding by pressing his forearms against his thighs. McKenzie brought towels from a rack to use pressure to try to ease the blood flow. He was trembling.

"Boris," he whispered. "Help Boris."

Another man wearing a white Giants jacket lay still in a puddle of blood on the floor next to a treadmill.

Edward was pressing a towel to his neck.

She knelt down to ask Frederic, "What happened? Help is coming."

"How is he?" Frederic asked faintly. The white towels were already drenched with blood. His face was as white as the towels.

She asked Frederic again, "What happened? Do you know who did this?"

"Boris screamed. I jumped out of the water and ran into this room," Frederic gasped. "He moved away from Boris to lunge at me. I...I...how do you say that? I jumped away. For a while I was too quick for him."

"You dodged away."

"I dodged. He was slashing out at me. I held my arms up for protection. He caught me. The sound of the janitor coming saved my life."

"Did you recognize anything about the attacker?" Jaden asked.

The dancer shook his head, pressing harder on the blood soaked towel on his arms. "He wore a knitted hat with eyes only showing. He could have been anyone. I kept my eyes on the knife, praying to save myself from that terror."

Jaden lowered her voice to almost a whisper. "What color was the knife?"

Frederic closed his eyes tightly. Jaden saw tears obviously caused by the pain. His head dropped back. She thought he was going to pass out. "Red handle. The blade was dark gray, no shiny steel. No. White. Small. Deadly. Razor…sharp." He forced out those last whispered words.

He's described the special edition Gideon stolen from my store! The murderer had to be someone who was in her shop the morning the company members visited.

Edward said, "Boris is still breathing. Barely." He put another towel under the man's left side. "The attack came from behind. Amateur. He still turned to try to defend himself. Sharp knife. Sliced right through the jacket. Frederic saved his life by diverting the killer. Jaden, could you call and make certain the paramedics know how seriously he is wounded?"

"The jacket must have protected him some. Not like Frederic," Jaden swallowed hard to force down her growing nausea at the sweet stench of blood,

Edward grabbed more towels. "Got to stop the neck bleeding. Pressure is all I can do. Those arm wounds look terrible, but

Frederic is in a lot better shape than this Boris." He shook his head.

Jaden ended her 911 call. "They have a crew in front of the hotel right now. They will be here in minutes. I told them exactly where we were." Tears rolled down her face.

Vision blurred by tears, she looked up to see a uniformed emergency medical technician rushing into the room with another man right behind.

"Oh, my God!" came from Nicolas Kurloff, who suddenly appeared in the room and sank down next to the gravely injured Boris, muttering in Russian.

The EMT ordered, "Sir, you'll have to get back."

"My dancers!" Nicolas protested.

"He's badly wounded but still alive," The med tech responded.

Nicolas finally noticed Frederic. "Oh, Frederic! Your arms! Oh, my beautiful dancers! It was the madman who killed my brother! Why! Why do they hate my dancers! What is happening?"

Another technician gently helped Nicolas to his feet. "Sir, please stay back."

Jaden and McKenzie led Nicolas to the side of the room. "They'll help him."

"Who has done this and why?" The man looked at them pleadingly. "Frederic has never been injured. Do you know that? He has a perfect dancer's body."

Frederic peered up at them with an ironic smile, "I have been lucky in my life until today."

You are still lucky. You are not Boris, Jaden thought bitterly. Her mind whirled. Do they hate the dancers? Either someone was just plain crazy or they did hate the dancers or the company.

Two of the medics were working on Boris and another rushed over to the white faced Frederic. He turned the dancer's arms and applied more pressure with white cloths or bandages that came out of his bag. Frederic winced. His whole body trembled.

"Deep wounds. You'll need stitches. Sir, you will be sent to the emergency room. Can you give a description of the attacker?"

Frederic shook his head. "A ski mask covered his face. I kept my eyes on the knife. All I could do was put my arms up."

One of the emergency crew asked, "Could you please leave the room? It will be easier to work without so many people. Did one of you report this? Thank you very much. The faster these wounds are treated the better."

Frederic was speaking hoarsely, "Another man came in. A cleaning man, I think. He frightened the killer so he ran into the hall. The cleaning man did not stay. He used the emergency phone on the wall. Very fast. Spoke the hotel address."

"911" McKenzie guessed. "Saved you."

"The man probably did not want anything to do with the police" Edward said. "We can easily find out who does the cleaning here. Maybe he noticed something different about the man. As crazed as he appears to be, he did not attack the janitor. The dancers were his target."

"Ma'am," One of the paramedics was speaking to her. "Ma'am, you'll have to leave them to us. Thanks for your help."

She saw that paramedics had already replaced McKenzie and Edward. Nicolas was being led, protesting, out into the crowd in the hallway.

Company members were questioning him in Russian, and he responded in an agitated voice. Jaden knew that Edward would understand the conversations.

As they moved into the hall, Edward speculated in a whisper. "The wound could have been self-inflicted. But where is the knife? I looked for it."

Jaden offered, "The attacker could have used something besides a knife."

Bill walked over to one of the med techs who was on duty tonight and was speaking to him quietly.

He turned to them. "Frederic will be all right. He does need stitches in one arm for certain and maybe both. And a transfusion. They will also give him something for the pain. It will probably knock him out for tonight. He can be interviewed after that. We'll try to keep this out of the news."

Because Boris was more critically injured he was sent to the hospital first. He was unconscious the entire time that they were with him.

I'm certain the knife came from my store! That beautiful, graceful knife could turn deadly. The murderer had to be someone who was in A Slice of Carmel the morning the company members were there.

"The slashes on each of his arms match," Edward said. "He could not have done that himself unless he can completely his nerves and has the accuracy of a genius. He could have cut one arm. But by then he would have been bleeding profusely. His right arm took the deepest cut. I think that means that the attacker was left handed."

"Unless he slashed backhanded."

"Thank you for giving us two choices, Jaden," Edward smiled weakly, staring at the blood-soaked arms of his worn jacket.

Jaden's heart thumped heavily as the emergency crew wheeled Frederic out on a gurney. She heard cries from the crowd in the hall as she had when Boris was wheeled out. The current residents of the hotel were mostly members of the company and understandably, visibly upset.

She sank to a chair while McKenzie and the Monterey detective spoke. "One, or maybe more, of the people in this dance company is a killer."

As much as Jaden wished it were not true, she realized they were correct. All along she had felt that the killer used the knife from her store, the knife that was stolen the morning members of the Kurloff company crowded in.

"Tell me what happened," came Edward's familiar voice from an unkempt old man that Jaden wanted to scold. His military posture was unmistakable now.

She turned to face him. "Edward! You were following us!"

Edward's face colored. "Guilty."

"Why?"

"We wanted to make certain nothing happened to either of you. Bobbi thought you might suspect her if she went down to the parking lot because there are so few homeless women.".

"Edward Stennis?" McKenzie's voice rose. "You suspected danger?"

"Yes," Edward answered. "There's a clever murderer wandering around here. We were trying to protect the wrong people."

"Someone wanted to kill Frederic." Jaden sensed she was right..

"Why do you think that?" McKenzie asked, a frown deepening on his forehead.

"Because Boris was wearing Frederic's jacket and probably his baseball cap. He was wearing them when he and Bill had a meeting. I'm sure the cap was to hide his hair. He was proud of his jacket, as he said, *'the team does well.'* Bill told me how proud he seemed to be of the Giants souvenirs. For some reason he loaned the jacket and hat to Boris. The killer wanted Frederic. I'm sure of that." Jaden felt a light, shaky touch on her arm.

A pale faced Maria was suddenly standing right next to her.

"What has happened?" the dancer asked in a trembling voice.

"Maria," Jaden spoke quietly hoping no one else in the hallway would hear. "Someone attacked Boris and Frederic in the exercise room."

Maria became visibly unsteady. Edward grabbed her arm.

"Please, I beg you." She steadied herself by pushing her hand against the wall. "Would you come to my room? The number is 340. One flight up. It is too dangerous here to talk out here, please."

"Yes, Maria. We'll come up. I want to wait first to call the hospital to find out about the condition of Frederic and of Boris. I'm very worried. Boris is more seriously hurt. He was stabbed in his side."

Maria gasped. She closed her eyes.

Edward spoke to her in Russian. Jaden caught one word-Frederic.

"I'm telling her that Frederic is in pain but in better condition than Boris."

"I understand. Will they be all right?" Maria's voice rose "They must be all right.

Come soon." She whirled away from them and disappeared in the crowd in the hall.

Jaden finally thought of calling Bill.

"Both of the dancers were stabbed?"

"I think that Frederic was the target. Boris was wearing the Giant's jacket and hat that you described to me. I'm not sure if he is going to make it. He lost a lot of blood."

"Sounds bad. I'll ask to put them in protective custody. I'll go over to the hospital as soon as I can."

"He did not recognize the killer because he was wearing a ski mask. Frederic was too busy trying to save himself."

"Jaden, I'll find out when I can interview Frederic. I should have seen this as a possibility. We may have a serial killer who hates dancers. I was too busy suspecting Frederic. Forgot the first rule. Everyone is a suspect. Please be careful. The person we want obviously knows the habits of everyone in the company."

"That cell phone you gave Frederic probably saved their lives."

"At least that's something," Bills voice was an angry growl.

"I will be careful. Keep me informed, won't you, Bill?"

"Of course."

"Oh, Maria wanted to see us. We are going to her room now." She started to move toward the stairs, thinking back to when her own involvement in this mystery began. That morning in the shop, crowded with dance company members, replayed in her mind. She met almost all of them.

Jaden should have done this earlier. Grandpa taught her to block out everything before she threw the knives. "Take a deep breath, Jaden." She heard his soothing voice. "Block our everything except what you want to do with that knife at that moment. The knife will obey you."

She should have done this earlier. That day in the store. Maria at the shop door.

Several others paused to look at the knife display. Maria, though, was the only person wearing a big, floppy smock made of teal blue silk that Jaden admired..

She almost ran up the stairs to the third floor. Jaden followed the arrow to rooms 324-340.

"Here it is," McKenzie said when they reached the end of the hall.

Jaden took a deep breath. She reached out her hand and pushed the slightly opened door. "Maria! It's Jaden! I'm with McKenzie Anderson and Edward Stennis."

The room was silent.

"Maria! It's all right," Edward spoke in a more commanding military tone.

"You told Jaden you wanted to talk to her. Are you in the bathroom? We'll wait out here."

Jaden knocked on the bathroom door. "Maria!" No noise. No sound of a person walking. "She asked us to come."

"It does not sound like there is anyone here. Jaden, would you check the bathroom? I'll check the closet," Edward peered into the small closet.

She knocked on the bathroom door. When there was no answer Jaden turned the knob. "No one." With one hand she pulled back the shower curtain. She turned to leave when she saw a purse hanging on the door hook partly hidden by a bath towel. Jaden did not want to touch it right now as she was beginning to feel more and more frightened. Maria could still be in the hotel somewhere.

"Why would she not close her door?"

Edward Stennis called, "I've found something. Here, Jaden."

Edward was holding a torn page that he showed to them. Jaden was certain the writing on the paper was Russian.

"Can you read that?" she asked Edward.

"Yes. It says, 'I'm sorry."

"She's sorry?" What does that mean?" McKenzie asked.

"She's sorry." Edward stared into space. He held up the note. "This paper was torn from something else. She's sorry she was late? She's sorry she ate too much?"

"If she's sorry for something, I think I can guess," Jaden said. "I don't think the note has anything to do with what she actually did. I think someone else left it."

"Where is she then?" McKenzie questioned. "She must be in the hotel."

"If someone left that note here, they may have taken her or she went willingly with her or him. Edward, we have to find her. Do you think we could ask the police to watch for Maria?" Jaden felt a pall in this room. She sensed that it was Maria's feelings. Downstairs the woman had been frightened. Here the dancer was terrified. "And Edward, I feel something important here in this room. I believe it should be searched."

"I agree. The police are so busy with the stabbing, though, that I don't know if anyone can come up. The room should be sealed and the maid needs to stay out. We should not touch anything, either. We don't have any evidence to justify doing that."

Just as he said that Jaden found something she wanted to touch. There was a notepad by the phone on the bedside table. She thought that there were some markings on the white paper. "Edward, do you see that notepad? There's some impressions on it. Can I try to bring out what was written there with a pen or pencil?"

Edward nodded. "You can do it without touching the pad or the pen that's there."

Jaden nodded. She pulled her evening bag from her pocket and fished inside.

Finally she drew out her pen.

"Good," Edward said. "You can rub the paper without touching the pad. Try it."

As Jaden scribbled over the markings, a number appeared. "It's local."

'We need one of those crisscross directories." Jaden slipped her pen back into her bag. "And I know how I can find one."

She dropped her pen in her bag and pulled out her cell phone. When her fingers brushed by her small knife, she pulled her monarch out and put it in her pocket where she could reach it in seconds.

She dialed the library reference desk.

Bobbi answered. "Harrison Memorial Library Reference. How may I help you?"

"It's Jaden, Bobbi. I can't take the time to tell you everything that's happened tonight right now. Could you help me?"

"Of course. What is it? I can tell by your voice that's something's really wrong. Are you all right? Are you hurt?"

"Yes. I mean, no. I'm not hurt," Jaden heard her own voice shaking. She swallowed hard, unable to tell Bobbi what had happened.

After a few seconds hesitation she gave her phone to Edward. "Please tell her what happened." Her voice croaked out in a harsh whisper. She cleared her throat.

Edward took the phone and explained the attack to Bobbi.

McKenzie slipped his arm over Jaden's shoulders. She grabbed a Kleenex from her pocket and wiped her eyes. *I should have known,* Jaden thought. I should have known. "I'm all right. May I speak to her again?"

"Jaden wants to tell you something." Edward explained, handing the phone back.

"Bobbi, there's a phone number that I'd like you to check in the criss-cross directory. I found that number here in Maria's room. It's the only clue we have. Could be nothing. Besides Frederic and Boris I'm worried about her. She asked us to meet her here and then disappeared. Is it possible for you to match that number with an address? The number does not look like a cell phone."

"Let me check. I'll call you back."

Bobbi hung up. Jaden looked down at her phone and saw the worst possible two words, "Battery low." She groaned out loud.

"What's the matter?" McKenzie asked.

"The battery is low on my cell phone."

"That's O.K. I have mine," McKenzie said. "And you have one, don't you, Edward? I'll call Bobbi and tell her to call me until you can get home and recharge it."

"Thanks, McKenzie."

During the conversation Edward patted his pocket. "Good thing you have one, McKenzie. I left mine in the apartment. I can't believe it, but when I put on this outfit my phone did not come with me. Well, No use staying here."

Jaden took one last look around the empty hotel room. "What she wanted to tell us was so important. Why didn't she stay here? Something's wrong. I think she knew something that would put her in danger. Maria was frightened."

"I agree." Edward left the door open a crack, just the way they had found it.

"Without more proof, what can we tell anyone? There's not a sign that anything happened to her. The police aren't going to search unless we give them a good reason."

"Why don't we have some coffee?" McKenzie suggested. "Maybe we can figure something out, or Bobbi will have a good lead for us."

"Look at that window open at the end of the hall." Edward walked away from them. "I'm going to check around there. See where it leads. I'll catch up with you."

As they started back down the stairs, they met a police officer. "Are you Jaden Steele and McKenzie Anderson?" he asked.

"Yes," McKenzie answered.

"You were the ones who found the injured dancers?"

"Yes, officer. Can we help you?"

"Lieutenant Cooper would like to speak to you. Can you come with me?"

"Of course," Jaden answered, glancing over her shoulder. Edward had disappeared.

She exchanged a glance with McKenzie. He nodded. They understood each other. If we have to be interviewed, at least Edward is free to do some investigation. He's free to call Bobbi, too, and ask about the address of that local phone number.

While they were going to meet Lt. Cooper, Edward stepped out of the window onto the rooftop of the old building.

The asphalt and gravel of the flat top roof crunched under his shoes as he walked to the edge of the building. The roof of the neighboring building, also flat topped, butted onto this one. The next roof beyond that did the same thing. No problem at all, even for an inexperienced second story man, to escape this way and travel at least three buildings away in minutes. These were old fashioned buildings with windows that opened. He breathed in the cool night air as he looked over the roofs of the city to the dark water of the bay. Strains of Christmas carols drifted up from a restaurant or business below. A fantasy of colored

Christmas lights twinkled everywhere on the buildings and on the boats in the harbor. Evil had destroyed the Christmas spirit here. This time of the year Santa should be running around the roof, not a killer.

"I'll search this roof first," Edward told himself. He wondered how the police interview with Jaden and McKenzie was going. He slipped out because he understood that Jaden wanted him free to do what he could to investigate the area.

If the police caught him on this roof he would be a prime suspect in the attack.

Edward used the small penlight on his key ring to begin to search the roof foot by foot. The only evidence he found was that the roof was an obvious haven for seagulls.

Nothing here.

Edward watched as the emergency vehicles pulled away from the hotel into the street. He kept searching for half an hour. The emergency vehicles pulled into the traffic, sirens wailing.

Speculations gushed through his mind. Jaden and McKenzie must be free by now. I can't take the chance of calling them. If the questioning officer were really sharp, he or she would have confiscated their cell phones by now.

I'll just keep on searching.

There were three roofs to search. After that, the person or the person with Maria would have to go down through a building and onto Alvarado Street.

It's going to take me a couple of hours. I'll have to search all three rooftops. If only I had better light. There's a murderer somewhere in the dark.

There's a killer loose. I might meet him or her any minute.

If Maria went with him willingly she's a fool. Now she knows what he or she is. That's what she wanted to tell us. Unlike the murderer, Maria has a conscience. The sociopath either kidnapped the ballerina or has killed her by now. He wished he could banish that thought. He had too much experience with terrorists and hired killers who did not have remorse for their victims.

Edward continued his back and forth investigation in the dimness. The lights of the city surrounding him helped. Searching the hotel roof took forty-five minutes. The only sign he found was a slight scuff mark on the two foot rise that butted up to the next building. By the time he searched the roof of the next building he had a sore neck from looking down. He was tired, hungry, and cold. In the old days he would have loved it.

Edward stopped and rubbed the right side of his neck. What am I doing up here?

"This is a waste of my time," he muttered. Suddenly he felt like laughing at himself. How furious he was when his superior told him that he was getting a little long in the tooth for fieldwork. That was from a person who rarely left his computer, who lived in a virtual world and thought everything could be solved by email directives. He kept on tonight just to spite his old boss.

That guy would probably end up with four stars because he played the political game. Edward tried. After years he realized how unhappy it made him to be a yes man.

When his mother became the target of a killer he came right out to Carmel.

What a great retirement area, he thought. He loved walking on the beach, watching the ever changing waves. So easy to forget about the sharks in the water.

Now he felt like he was sleepwalking. That was one clever killer. Not a sign. Not a clue. When Edward saw a patch of white in a vent, he stared. He raised the pen light to the white object. The closer he got, the more his heart accelerated. The object was a towel. And the towel had blood stains on it. The attacker had no doubt been in a hurry.

He thought he had stuffed the towel and possibly the knife into the vent. Because of the housing over the vent Edward could not look down into the pipe.

Is it your first mistake? Maybe your second. The writing pad that Jaden had noticed and I did not might trap you. You probably used gloves in the attack in the exercise room, and Igor's murder, and the homeless woman. If you discarded those gloves here you may have left a fingerprint on the inside. Maybe the knife, too, although you may still want to use it.

Edward finished checking the roof until he came to a rooftop door that led to a stairway. This is how Maria and her kidnapper walked down. He was certain of that. The killer knows this area better than a tourist would. He or she is local.

This third floor was all empty business offices. The second floor, too. Perfect for escape. The only person one might find would be a custodian at this time of night. He smelled food cooking, though. Spicy.

He could hear strains of middle-eastern music echoing up the stairs. He passed the women's and men's restrooms that were no doubt used by the customers of the restaurant below. The set up for casually walking out of the crowded restaurant was almost ideal.

Now, where could he find a pay phone? Were there any pay phones anymore?

He could not charge a call to his credit card. That would be as bad as using his own cell phone. Edward took off his battered old hat to wipe his brow. He sank to the edge of a bus stop bench when a hand reached out toward him.

"Here, pops," a voice came out of a group waiting to get into the Song of Arabia.

"Get yourself a cup of coffee."

Edward looked into his hat.

Four quarters.

Another hand dropped in a dollar.

He grinned. Finally, he laughed out loud. People were staring at him and backing away from the crazy old man. Edward was too numb to care.

Ask and ye shall receive.

McDonalds was just two blocks down the road.

They must have a pay phone.

Maria took the tea with trembling hands.

"Drink it," he said. "You will feel much better. It's warm."

His Russian was not bad. It was awkward, of course, like her English.

"I did not understand why you wanted the beautiful red knife." The steam from the hot tea wafted into her nose. She took a sip. It did make her feel better. "You killed Igor and tried to kill Frederic and Boris. Why?"

"Igor was an evil man. Frederic, Frederic had to die, too. Stabbing Boris was a mistake. He was in my way. Anyone in my way has to be dealt with. Anyone who crosses me has to be dealt with."

Maria shivered. She would never have guessed that this gentle looking man was a killer. She took another large sip of tea. Igor was evil. She could believe it of that man. There was a lot in his past that might create hatred. His own wife did not like him. But this man was consumed by hatred.

She drank the whole cup of tea and he made another for her. In spite of the hot brew, Maria felt cold inside. The cold was fright. She realized that she was in his way.

Why else would he have insisted that they leave the hotel? He took her out the window onto the roof. They crossed over two other buildings. All of the buildings had vents, pipes, sticking out. He picked one and stuffed in a white towel with bloodstains and some other things, including the knife. She heard it clatter at the bottom of the pipe.

"You see," he spoke soothingly. "The knife is gone now, Maria. You are safe."

The more she thought, the more she realized that safety was a dream. He knew that she wanted to speak to Jaden Steele and her friends. That promise to marry her so she could stay in the states was a lie. His mind was deranged.

All she wanted to do was escape.

Maria edged toward a window. They were on the second story very near the ocean. If he would only leave the room, she might be able to climb out. She was a fast runner and in much better condition than he. Why did she ever trust him?

He stared at her in a peculiar, detached way. The chill mushroomed inside of her cramping stomach. The hot tea turned to ice.

She shivered again.

"You are cold. Drink more of your tea." He pulled a plaid wool blanket from a chair to put around her shoulders.

"Would you like to lie down?" He gently led her to the bedroom.

Maybe he would leave her alone in there. She could still escape.

She sat down on the edge of the bed. Her eyelids felt heavy and her head groggy.

"You rest," he spoke so quietly.

Maria realized that she was unusually tired. This was not like her. She must get away. Why didn't I tell the police what I knew about Igor's murder? Her head began to throb. Her stomach hurt. She could not stop a yawn. He took her shoes off and lifted her suddenly useless legs to the bed.

"Maria. You were going to talk to Jaden Steele and McKenzie and Edward. You are in my way. I can't allow anyone to be in my way. If only I could have trusted you."

"You lied. Your promise....." Her eyes would not open. She felt tears on her face and turned toward the bed to try to wipe them away.

"I did not lie, Maria. I promised that you would stay in America and you will."

The phone by the bed rang. She tried to move her arm toward it. *No use.* She knew now what a mistake she had made.

She heard him answer the phone with "Hello." After that he did not speak.

The last sound Maria heard was the telephone crashing to the floor.

All sounds were far away now, as though she were miles from this nightmare.

The telephone did not fall. Someone threw it.

At seven a.m. Bill stepped out of his Carmel black and white in the parking lot of CHOMP, Community Hospital of the Monterey Peninsula. Hospital Information had told him that Frederic would be able to talk to him. The famous dancer was given a sedative in order to have a good night's sleep after both of his arms were stitched. Bill was already speaking to the Monterey Police Department about a guard for Frederic and for Boris. There might not be word on Boris' condition until late today.

Bill walked past the indoor pond that made the hospital so relaxing to the first floor wing. Hoping that Frederic could talk to him, he looked for room 155. Ahead of him he saw a hospital security guard who was already checking visitors. Bill took out his badge and identification.

"Go ahead, sir," the guard told him. "I was already told that you were coming."

"Thank you for checking me," Bill said. "The man in 155 is in danger."

"I was already told. Plus, people have been steadily calling the switchboard about him. He has a lot of fans and newspapers and television. They all want to see him."

Bill answered, "They have to be kept out. Do the best you can. I know how famous he is and how demanding some reporters can be. Someone from the Monterey Police Department should be over here soon to keep the buzzards at bay."

"That will help," the security guard answered. "We are not a large city hospital."

Bill headed into 155. A nurse was just finishing taking Frederic's blood pressure.

When he spotted Bill, Frederic's dark eyes sparkled in a pale face.

"Bill. Hello," he said quietly. "Do you know anything about Boris?"

"No, Frederic. Not yet. Possibly this evening. He is in critical condition."

Frederic sighed deeply. "What is happening? I don't understand."

The nurse spoke to Bill. "Try not to upset him too much. He's been through a real trauma. His blood pressure is high. He needs as much rest as he can get. He's been given medication that will make him drowsy. His words will be slurred."

"I understand," Bill pulled the one chair in the room next to the bed. "There are some important questions that I need to ask him."

"I will help you. Whatever I can do."

"You did not recognize the attacker?"

"No," Frederic answered slowly. "There was something, just for a second, that made me think of someone. Then I was trying to get him away from Boris and save myself. No time for deep thoughts. He was not a dancer. My heart is still racing."

"You said someone, Frederic. Who?" Bill thought briefly about hypnosis, but the man was still weak and sedated.

"I can't think of it but I will soon." His voice was sounding huskier.

Bill knew that he must hurry.

"Frederic. We still have not heard from Gene. Do you know where he is?"

The dancer nodded.

"You do?"

"He has not run away or been kidnapped. He is afraid. Gene has always been, ah, how do you say? Shy? Easily frightened. Takes things to heart. The murders terrified him. He has just stayed at home. Since he has a post office box he does not give out his address. I give him a home in my building. He is my only family."

Bill slowly realized, "He lives in one of your apartments."

"Yes. Gene lives there, above the restaurant. Few know."

"When did you last see him, Frederic?"

"When he gave me the note for you. He did not want people to worry."

"So you have not heard from him in a week? Would you give me permission to go into Gene's apartment? Are there extra keys? Maybe you have them in your room?"

"Yessinia has the keys in a desk in the restaurant's office. If I call her now, she will give them to you. Why do you want to see Gene's apartment? Do you think something is wrong? Has something happened to him?"

"Possibly," Bill answered quietly. "Just a routine check, Frederic. There's one more thing. Jaden thought that the sight of the old woman in the Fishermen's Wharf parking lot upset you? Is she right? Did you know the woman?"

"I knew it could not be true. For a few seconds she looked like my mother."

Edward called Bobbi's cell phone with the information that he knew.

"Any luck with the number?"

"Yes. I have the address. 1125 Lighthouse Avenue in Pacific Grove. I've been trying to call Jaden. Where is she?"

"I think the battery on her cell was low. The police were questioning her and McKenzie. They must be done by now. It has to be about one a.m. My car's in the Pacific Avenue parking lot. It will take me a few minutes to walk over there and then I'll be home. I hope mom's not worried."

"You are sixty-five, Edward."

"I could be ninety and my mother would still worry about me."

She laughed. "It's strange. I called that number Jaden gave me. The voice sounded so familiar. 'Hello' was the only word he said. Then I asked if I could speak to the woman of the house. I heard a noise and the line went dead."

"You can't identify the voice yet?"

"No. it will probably come to me about three in the morning."

"Thanks Bobbi. Was that 1125 Lighthouse? I might drive by there."

"I'm going to try to get into property tax records to see who owns the property." Bobbi added.

"That's a good idea," Edward agreed before he hung up.

Jaden should be home by now, Edward thought as he trudged up Del Monte.She was with McKenzie. He would take care of her.

On his right was the wharf area and the yacht harbor and Fisherman's Wharf. Both areas and most of the other businesses in town were decorated with multicolored lights in honor of the season. The background of the black ocean accented their brilliance.

"Tis the season to be jolly. I could be happier if the murderer were caught. Well, I am happy that I'm out of Washington, D.C. Thank you for that, Santa Claus, wherever you are."

At Frederic's café Bill caught Yessinia just as she was closing for the night. The news about Frederic made her bury her head in her hands and begin to cry. "Why would anyone do that? He is such a beautiful dancer and Boris, too. Frederic also is such a nice boss. Of course I only see him once a year or so. Gene always takes the rent payments and sees that problems are fixed."

"Have you seen Gene today?"

"No. I have not." She wiped her eyes with a handkerchief.

"Yessinia, you can go home. I'll look upstairs myself if you don't object."

"Don't try to re-enter here or the alarm will go off." The woman nodded, picked up her purse, and left the building.

Except for the hum of the refrigerator in the restaurant kitchen, there was no other sound in the building. Why didn't I think of this before? I never realized where Gene lived. He kept this a secret. He could have lived in the gallery for all Bill knew.

"Why didn't I ever ask?" Bill walked up the wooden steps to the two apartment doors on the landing. Frederic never mentioned another tenant. Maybe there was none. Why not? An apartment in this area would command a good rent. Yessinia said Gene's apartment was on the right. He knocked on the door. There was no stirring inside. Of course it must be around two a.m. Who would answer the door at this hour?

"Hello!" he called. "Police! Please open the door. Whoever is there, open the door!"

The key turned easily in the lock. Streams of artificial light from the neighboring buildings patterned the floor of Gene's apartment. Bill turned on the light. "Hello. Police."

A prickly feeling crept up the back of his neck. The door to the bedroom was open. Bill saw that the phone was on the floor. "Gene?" he said to the form in the bed.

As he walked closer he saw that the person was not Gene. Lying in the bed was the woman who had delighted the audience in the Dance of the Sugar plum Fairies. She was paler than ever now, as pale as the white sheets that covered her.

Bill now knew the explanation for her behavior at the hotel. He was sure she had stolen the knife from Jaden's store.

Maria was not breathing.

Had she taken her own life?

Retired General Edward Stennis saw the red flashing lights from two blocks away on Lighthouse Ave. He parked his car as soon as he found a space. There was no use trying to drive through that many police and emergency vehicles. It's the killer. He's always one step ahead of us. Why can't we trap him? Because he is clever and can behave normally.

Ahead of him he was certain he saw Bill speaking to another officer.

A policewoman came up to him and said, "Sir, you can't go any farther."

"Could I speak to that officer?" He pointed at Bill and cried out his name.

Bill looked toward him. He waved and yelled, "Edward! I'll be right over!"

He left the other officers and walked toward Edward.

"What's going on?" Edward already knew that whatever happened was bad.

Bill walked over to the side of the restaurant building. "It's Maria. She's dead."

Edward groaned to himself. *That beautiful young woman.*

"Oh, no. If only we had gone up to her room sooner! How did she die?"

"At first I thought she killed herself. So far we think he gave her barbiturates. Then he held a pillow over her face."

"We might have seen the murderer. We might have saved her." Edward slumped against the plate glass window of the Russian café.

"You would have run right into a killer unarmed. He might have killed you if he thought you were in his way."

"You're right, of course, Bill. I'm almost positive that he disposed of the knife."

"There was no sign of him. Just the phone on the floor. The cord was pulled out of the wall. He lived here. I really never asked where Gene lived," Bill told him.

Edward began to explain how he had spent the evening. "The work was worth it.

I finally found that bloody towel stuck on the vent. I'm almost positive that there is more evidence down there. Someone in the Monterey Police Force has to get a warrant to open that vent pipe. With all this going on they may not have had the time. Or maybe they thought I was a crank."

"If I call Lt. Cooper he will get to work on it. I'll check right now." Bill brought out his phone and pressed one button. Obviously he had his friend in his address book.

Edward's legs ached more than they had in thirty years of field work. He had trudged through desert sands and frozen in the arctic. He watched Bill talking to his friend on the cell phone. The apartment phone was on the floor and the cord pulled out of the wall.

Besides his legs his chest began to ache. The conversation he had with Bobbi leapt into his mind. "He only said one word, 'Hello,' but it sounded so familiar." Edward Stennis swallowed hard. He could not swallow the low growl that was coming from deep in his throat. "Bill." Maybe he was alarmed for nothing.

The sunrise to his right cast a red glow over the water of the bay. It was a cold, clear morning. A few gulls were beginning to patrol the beaches for another day.

His imagination was working overtime. His instincts knew that something was wrong. Where was Gene? Where would he go? The other place he could be was in the gallery in Dolores Court. This man somehow went completely out of control and started serial murder. Gene stayed a very private person. No one knew that he lived here. He went to a lot of trouble to keep his home a secret. Or, maybe no one ever asked where he lived.

"Bill," Edward tried to control his voice. "Bill, I know it's only around five-thirty. I need to call Bobbi."

Bill's dark eyes widened. "You think he might have gone over to the court?"

Edward nodded.

"You're right." He handed the phone to Edward. It rang at least a dozen times before Bobbi answered in a husky voice.

"Hello."

"Bobbi, this is Edward."

"Where are you? Esther will ask."

"I'm in Pacific Grove with Bill. Maria has been murdered. Stay in your apartment until we get there."

"All right," she answered in a whispered choke, as though someone had grabbed her throat and squeezed.

"That voice you heard say hello. Do you think that was Gene?"

"Oh, God. Yes. I should have recognized him right away."

Around three a.m. that morning Jaden watched as McKenzie turned the key in the lock of her apartment door. She could barely feel her hands and her feet. If she did not get to a bed soon she was going to fall over.

"I could come in and stay with you." McKenzie stood in the doorway.

"Thanks for bringing me home. I need to get some sleep. You must be as tired as I am. Why did the officers keep asking the same questions over and over?"

"Could be because you were involved in three murder cases."

"Right. I'll be fine with some sleep,"

"Sleep sounds like heaven. I'm obviously not as young as I used to be. It really shows."

"Good morning." Jaden was fighting to keep her eyes open.

"Jaden, I'll call you tomorrow afternoon. I'm sorry I may have to go back to San Diego because of a court date."

"Thanks, McKenzie. You've done so much already."

Jaden tried to move her numb fingers to unzip her dress. There seemed to be no connection between them and her brain. Finally she gave up, falling to the welcome bed, barely able to pull back the top sheet and blanket. She felt like ocean waves were trapped in her stomach. Before her evening bag fell to the carpet, she slipped her knife into her jacket pocket like a child would a comforting doll.

All night a thought like an elusive little fly had been buzzing around her mind.

She vainly tried to banish all her thoughts. She needed sleep. Sometimes those slippery little things came to her during sleep. It seemed like days since McKenzie picked her up for dinner. Maria wanted to see us. Why did she leave? *Someone forced her.* Jaden felt that deeply and was afraid for the vulnerable ballerina.

That person had to be the killer. Maria must have known. No sign of a struggle.

"No one is going to care if I sleep in my clothes," she mumbled to herself. "I'm too tired to even be sick." Jaden sat up for all of five seconds. She tipped to the right in slow motion until her head sank into the pillow. That was all that she remembered.

Her dreams of shadowy figures pounding on her door dissolved into heart racing nightmares.

All of the nightmare figures brandished knives of a hundred different colors. They stabbed at the door like a grotesque rainbow. One of them was wearing a black tuxedo. He grew taller and skinnier until he was barely a slit holding a graceful red handled Gideon knife. Suddenly she realized who the murderer could be.

Reaching for her phone, Jaden fought to open her eyes to escape the throbbing in her head. A streak of light fell over her eyes. She opened them to slits. The bright light filled with swirling flecks of dust actually hurt. She closed her eyes. *I escaped those stabbing ghouls.* The light should make her want to get up. A groggy fog had invaded her body. Jaden moved her fingers first. They proved to be cooperative.

What time is it?

She rolled over to open her eyes again to stare at the clock. Six-fifteen! *I thought I would sleep until noon at the least.*

Her nightmare of the stabbing ghosts dissolved in the morning light. The one piece that was missing from the puzzle fell into the right spot. She saw the murderer's face in the demonic crowd. The face of the one person who somehow changed clothes during the premier evening appeared before her in the middle of the demons. The last piece of the puzzle fell into place.

I have to call Bill! It does not seem possible. I know who the murderer is and can guess why.

She reached for the phone on the bed table to call Bill. It was gone. Could she have knocked it on the floor last night? She felt on the floor for the phone or her bag. It was gone, too. A sudden cold feeling like the return of the nightmare paralyzed her for a moment. The phone! Where was it? The cold nightmare engulfed her when she heard someone in the room.

"You are not going to find your phone," a familiar voice said in a hard, cold whisper.

"What are you doing in here?" She already knew what he was doing or what he was planning. She bluffed, "Get out!"

Gene laughed. The eerie laugh made Jaden sink back down to the bed.

I've never heard him laugh. He always had a sad look about him. He's been secretly laughing at us all this time. Why did it take me this long to figure it out? As soon as I knew he was Frederic's cousin that should have been enough to suspect.

He has been smarter than the rest of us.

There aren't many motives. Money is a big one. Love. Jealousy. Hate.

"I am going away," he answered, smiling. "You are going with me."

For the first time she saw that he was holding a gun. "I...I...." She stared at the barrel of the small gun. Knives she knew. Guns she didn't. It was small. Deadly enough. And he might keep her alive for a while, but not forever.

"You should have a lock on your kitchen window. Bobbi does. With that balcony on the outside of these three apartments, it is so easy to walk around to find a window to open. I lifted your window out."

"That's very clever of you, Gene. You had us all fooled. Even Frederic."

"Frederic, the brilliant dancer. Always in the news. Women. Money to buy property and a business in Pacific Grove. Money to finance the gallery."

"He did a lot for you."

"I am some charity because I am his cousin. He pays the lease on the gallery. He gives me an apartment above his restaurant. He has that perfect dancer's body. He stayed with his mother until she died. All the women he wants. Every time I saw his picture in those newspapers I tore it up. Then he joined the company of the man I hated more than anything in the world."

"Igor Kurloff."

"On one of the company's American tours he took my mother away. He said he would marry her and they would come back for me. She left me a note. A note!"

He spat out the last two words, then started to laugh again. "She disappeared. I had to live with foster families. Some were cruel. My mother never returned. I knew Igor killed her."

"You've been waiting, plotting all these years for revenge."

"Yes. I could not believe my good luck when the academy received a letter saying the company wanted to perform in the new Monterey Performing Arts Center. "

"Bad luck for Igor."

"Because of the children I went to many rehearsals to study the schedules and the backstage timing. No one paid attention to me when I left the audience. Igor begged for his life. He said he left my mother alive. Igor claimed he told her, 'Go back to your son.' Swore he did not harm her. I would never have been caught except for Frederic."

"Frederic?" Jaden slipped her hand in her pocket and fingered the Monarch.

"When he took you out, he came back and told me about the homeless woman. For a second he thought he had seen his own mother. I could not believe what he said and had to see for myself. The years were cruel, but it was her."

With dawning horror Jaden realized what Gene had done. "But it was her sister, your mother."

"Yes." Gene spit out the word. "I knew it was her. She was old and ugly. She lived here all those years and never returned for me. She wanted to be a drunk and a derelict, like the scum on the waves."

Jaden felt sick. Now she knew what pushed Gene Miller into a mad, murdering spree. For years he thought Igor had murdered his mother. Then he found out that she deserted him for a bottle. No doubt she became mentally ill after Igor deserted her. If only she had gone back to her son.

Jaden whispered, "Where is Maria?"

Gene did not answer. He was staring beyond Jaden's shoulder. Finally he shook his head. "Maria is at my apartment."

The way he said the words made her tremble...she closed her eyes.

He went on, "We were together when Bobbi called. I knew somehow she suspected me or she would not have called. I tried to get into her apartment. None of the windows would open. Yours...I knew if Bobbi suspected me you did, too. You are friends. You talk together." He looked beyond her out the window into a space that only he could see.

"I know. Maria stole the knife for you, didn't she, Gene?"

"Yes. She gave it to me right away in the alleyway by the door to the garage. I told her I wanted to frighten Igor because of how cruel he was to my mother. She was such a fool. Maria thought I would marry her so she could stay in the States. How stupid."

"Gene. Let me call Bill. He can help you. He is your good friend. You sell his paintings. You both like art so much."

Gene lifted the gun barrel so it pointed toward her. "We are not calling anyone. They will put me in jail. We are going outside. You are going to disappear. Let people wonder about you."

"Gene. Please."

"Walk out your door. Stay close to me. We are going to go in my car."

"I don't want to go."

"You will go or I will shoot you right here. Then I will wake up Bobbi and shoot her and the old woman and shoot her."

"I'll do what you say, Gene. Don't hurt them. Please. You can't kill everyone."

He tossed her black flat shoes toward the bed. One fell on the floor.

"Put them on. We would not want you to get cold." He chuckled.

Jaden shivered as though someone had just tossed her out into a snowstorm. She should have figured this out a lot sooner than too late. Her feet barely carried her out the door. The shoes felt like two huge rocks.

"Move, Jaden. Quick! We are going down the stairs and across the courtyard to my car."

She gulped air in several quick breaths and almost choked. "Gene. I'll do exactly what you want. Just tell me."

Her eyes shifted to the front window of Esther's apartment. *Empty.*

Praying for one thing, she forced herself to breathe deeply and slowly.

"Down the stairs!" Gene ordered, poking the gun into her back.

At the third step, Jaden hesitated slightly. Gene was one stair above her when a white streak blurred across his path down the stairs. The surprised man was knocked slightly sideways, flailing, grasping for the railing. In a second Jaden whipped out the blade of her knife and aimed directly for his chest. Instead, the sharp tip drilled into his right arm. His scream filled the air, followed by a blast from his gun. He fell, rolling the rest of the way down the concrete steps.

Jaden's ears echoed. She dashed down, frantically searching for the pistol. A glint by the base of the planter caught her eye. With shaking hands she scooped it up. The odor of gun smoke filled her nostrils. *I might be deaf.* Her ears were ringing. Her hands clutched the handle of the gun as she shakily pointed it directly at the moaning killer.

Blood poured from his forehead and from the slash on his arm.

He killed three people and would have killed more. *I can't let down my guard because he's hurt. He's more dangerous now than ever.*

Arizona sat proudly in the courtyard at the base of the stairs licking her paws, as if to crow, Beat you again! After carefully examining her paws, she stretched over to the rapidly spreading pool of blood and began to lick.

Though the concrete steps behind her were vibrating, Jaden would not turn to see who was coming down the stairs. She did not dare turn from the wounded man to see who was coming. If the person were an accomplice of the gallery owner, she was still in danger. Out of the corner of her eye, she caught sight of another gun barrel.

"Jaden!" Edward's voice echoed in the deserted Dolores Court. "My, God!"

Her hands trembled so violently that there was no way she could fire a gun. She felt like a frozen statue. Her heart finally slowed to a near normal pace. One of her ears popped and suddenly she could hear more sounds, including a siren.

Edward touched her shoulder. "I have him. It's O.K. You're safe. It's all right. Give me the gun."

She could not move. Her death grip on the pistol relaxed slightly. With trembling hands she lowered the gun in slow motion until the barrel pointed down toward the concrete.

Edward gently reached over to take the gun from her hand. He clicked the safety into place. "We wouldn't want to shoot holes in the flagstones, would we? Besides, the bullets might ricochet and hit us."

The sirens stopped.

Dolores Court was suddenly filled with a crowd that whirled in front of Jaden's eyes. Bobbi appeared next to her. "Edward, she's not hurt?"

"Gene," Jaden whispered. "He was insane. Completely insane. He wanted to kill us, too." Her legs would not hold her any longer. She leaned on the iron stair railing for support.

"We know," Edward answered. "We realized almost too late."

Bill ran into the court, gun drawn. He stopped in mid-stride when he saw Jaden, Edward, and Gene who was shaking his head, struggling to sit up.

"Gene!" Bill yelled. "Don't move!"

"Gene is the murderer."

Bill's mouth opened but no words escaped. He gripped his gun.

Another policeman entered from the alleyway from the parking garage. "I am a police officer! Put the guns down," he yelled at Edward, who immediately placed both guns on the patio stones.

"Jaden's safe, Dave!" Bill called back to the other officer. "The killer is down! I'm going to call and make certain an ambulance is prepared for his injuries." Bill used his cell phone for a minute, and then walked to Jaden's side.

He slipped his arm around her waist.

"Take some deep breaths."

She heard her own voice waver. "He was going to kill me and," her voice broke, "and Bobbi and Esther. He had lost his reason completely. I don't know how he learned that I suspected him. Frederic probably said something that made him realize."

Bobbi suddenly appeared next to them. "I think I know. When I called Gene he realized that I knew where he was. This was my mistake. I shouldn't have known his home number. Bill, can we take Jaden upstairs? She needs to sit down."

Jaden needed to lie down. Her legs were shaking and her ears echoed from the gunshot. The crowd in the court began to carousel around her until they disappeared.

She woke but for a few seconds did not know where she was. Not her bed in her Nebraska home...her apartment in Dolores Court in Carmel.

Someone was standing in the door frame. Jaden struggled to sit up. Her throat and mouth felt dry.

"Jaden. Sit up slowly, dear. You are safe. Everything is fine." Bobbi turned away for a second. "She's awake. Edward, would you call Bill? He wanted to know. He'll be right over."

She moved to Jaden and slipped an extra pillow behind her back. "Stay here for now," she ordered. "I'll get you some coffee."

Bobbi left the room while two people entered. No mistaking Frederic's graceful, athletic form accompanied by Esther.

The older woman hugged her. Edward came into the room carrying one of her dining room chairs. "Mom, sit here."

He set the chair down and moved to the bed to kiss Jaden on the forehead.

Bobbi returned with a tray with four steaming coffee mugs.

Though Jaden felt groggy the odor of the coffee helped clear her mind.

Bobbi said, "I'm sorry, Jaden. I realized what Gene had done too late."

"I did, too," Jaden responded in a hoarse whisper. "Everything fit together just as Gene broke in. Some detective I am."

Esther hugged her again and pulled the old wedding ring design quilt up to her neck.

"Bobbi, thank you." Jaden cradled the warm mug with both hands. The first hot sip warmed her and stopped the shivering. She cleared her throat. "How long have I been asleep?"

No one answered her.

"The sun is so bright. What time is it?" she asked.

"Noon," Bobbi finally answered.

"What day?"

"Tuesday," Esther told her.

"Tuesday! I only remember Monday morning about dawn when Gene broke into the apartment. I've slept for over twenty-four hours?"

Jaden heard Bill's voice as he entered the apartment without knocking or ringing the bell.

He came right into the bedroom to the side of the bed. "Jaden. I'm...I'm." He hesitated before he, too, kissed her lightly on the forehead.

Edward explained, "I brought a doctor over yesterday evening. After hearing everything that happened he advised letting you sleep."

"I feel like I've run a marathon."

"Don't get up until you feel like it," Esther said. "Hal is taking care of the shop."

A pale faced Frederic took a cup of coffee from Bobbi. His arms and neck were bandaged. "I want to thank you, ladies. My life is yours. My own cousin. I cannot believe what he did. He was my only living relative and I thought he was my friend. Gene started the gallery with my help. He never said one bad word to me. And yet he tried to kill me and attacked Boris and did kill Igor."

"He was jealous," Jaden explained. "Jealous to the point that he could no longer reason. He hated his mother for deserting him for Igor, who grew tired of her and threw her over when he returned to the old Soviet Union."

"After that happened she started to drink and never was able to go home to her son. Substance abuse put her on the streets. Either she was not capable or was too embarrassed. Gene went into the foster system." Bobbi continued, "Once Gene realized what had happened, he plotted revenge. He thought Igor killed his mother. Hatred simmered in him for years."

Jaden added, "It was an incredible coincidence that Frederic saw Gene's mother in the parking lot and commented to Gene on the resemblance. After all these years he casually told Gene that he imagined he had seen his mother as a beggar in the parking lot by the pier. That's what he told his cousin. If we had never gone to the wharf that evening, Gene's mother, your aunt, would still be alive. She was in a bad way, though, from drinking. She would not have lasted much longer. We are so lucky that Boris is recovering."

"It was my fault." Frederic gazed out of the window of Jaden's apartment. "Maria's death, too."

"Poor woman," Esther commented.

"No." Bill put his hand on Frederic's shoulder. "You are not at fault. Gene is the person responsible. He planned Igor's murder. He used a plastic poncho to protect himself. One was found in the trash backstage in the auditorium . He threw his gloves off the pier after both stabbings."

Frederic took a deep breath and winced, twisting his shoulders, and finally easing back in the chair. "My arms. They feel so sore. Gene had many chances to kill me."

Bill poured another cup of coffee. "He would have been the first suspect. He tried to make it look like a stranger was the killer."

"I put all the facts together too late," Jaden explained. "Something had been nagging at me for days. During the questioning at the Monterey Performing Arts Center, Gene mentioned Igor's stabbing. Bill had already cautioned us not to talk about the killing. Unless one of us blabbed, he should not have known how Igor died. And he appeared different from the start of the ballet to the end when he was wearing a topcoat."

Bill agreed, "We tried to not release that information about the stabbing."

Frederic stared at the floor. "He was different. Moody. Sometimes like, like, a completely different person. We kept the fact that we were cousins a secret because I thought that Gene would not want reporters to bother him."

Bill's face hardened. "Right now I'm trying to ignore the fact that you did not mention Gene was your cousin. He was staying in an apartment that you owned. And you two…."

If there were a way Jaden could have vanished from the room, she would have.

Bill's voice filled the room, "Did either of you think that piece of information provided a motive for the attempted killing of Frederic? Gene was free to murder. Jaden, you owe your life to a cat!"

Bobbi chimed in, "And her own quick thinking and skill with knives. Bill, can you wait until tomorrow to tell her everything that she did wrong? Look at how tired she still is. It's my fault, too. Edward put locks on my windows. Gene knew something was wrong when he heard my voice on the phone. We were trying to sort out the information. I never thought of the relationship being a motive. Greed. Jealousy. He wanted what his cousin had. In his mind you had everything…women, you were a famous dancer, you had the money to buy the business in Pacific Grove, and you financed the art gallery. He snapped. Except for seeing Frederic and Gene in First

Murphy Park, we did not have a lot of definites. Just guesses."

Bill took a deep, audible breath. His face softened. He nodded.

Jaden insisted, "I'm all right. I'll tell you what happened, Frederic Melinikov."

Frederic sat up suddenly, turning his head toward the women.

"Bobbi was trying to trace your family history online. It was really difficult because of the language problem and a different type of record keeping. She learned about your family. You and Gene were first cousins."

"It was a Russian name site that first gave me the idea. A common translation of Melnikov is Miller. Then I read that is a very common name in Russia," Bobbi said. "Gene Miller."

"Roberta, you are a very clever woman, as well as beautiful." He managed a weak smile.

Jaden and Bill smiled at each other. Frederic was returning to normal.

Maybe Dolores Court would return to normal, too, or as normal as the court could ever be.

They could use a little peace to sit back and listen to the ocean. Jaden longed to sit on the white sand beach, watch the seagulls gliding over the surf as they sentineled the waves in Monterey Bay.

"How could Gene do it, Jaden?" Hal asked after they opened the store on Monday morning a week after Gene had tried to kill her. It was Jaden's first day back.

"The hurt began when his mother deserted him for Igor. He grew up, but the pain overrode everything in his life, like a scab over a festering wound. In his mind Igor caused his mother to abandon him. On one of the company tours of America, they met. She filled in one of the parts in Swan Lake. She went away with him thinking he would marry her. Instead he deserted her. When Gene knew the company was performing here, he began to plan his revenge." Jaden stared at the last red handled Gideon in the display case. Just as she thought, it had been a good seller. Thankfully, the police never released the make of the deadly knife.

The phone rang. Hal answered and said, "It's for you. McKenzie."

With a shock Jaden realized that she had forgotten all about McKenzie. He had not come to see her all week and she had not thought about him.

So much had been going on. Different officers and detectives questioned her. Bill said she would have to testify at a Grand Jury hearing.

"Jaden," McKenzie said. "Are you all right? I'm sorry that I had to return to San Diego for a court date. I was committed to the defense. We've been preparing all week but I have exchanged emails with Bobbi."

"I understand, McKenzie."

"You or Bobbi let me know if I should plan to come back for any reason."

"Thank you. I appreciate that."

She hung up just as an older couple walked into the store.

The man paused to take out his wallet. He removed a slip of paper. "Your website says that you have one of the special holiday editions of the Gideon left."

Jaden and Hal exchanged a quick glance. Her voice vanished.

Hal answered, "Yes we do." He opened the display cases closest to the door and brought out a twin of the same deadly knife that had been used in the murders, the last of the holiday Gideons.

I hope it's not a red handle, Jaden thought, holding her breath.

But Hal brought out a twin of the same deadly knife that Maria had stolen, that Gene used to murder Igor and his own unfortunate mother.

She did her best to stifle a gasp.

Her muffled cry was drowned by the woman saying, "Ohhh, it's beautiful. The handle is so graceful. Very unusual."

Hal handed it to her, "It fits the hand perfectly. Try."

She took it and smiled.

The man said, "I think that's a yes." He brought out a credit card. "You have quite an inventory."

"Is there anything else I can show you?" Hal, always the salesman, asked as he swiped the credit card. "May I see your ID?"

The customer opened his wallet to show his driver's license. "This is enough for today. We would like to see what you have."

He and his wife wandered through the shop, pausing at the sword case. "These are really interesting. Is the one that says sold a confederate soldier's sword?"

"Yes," Hal answered.

"And that small knife with the bone handle. Why is that in the case?"

Jaden found her voice. "My grandfather made the knife."

"Actually," Hal offered, "that small knife is the most valuable item in the shop. Abel Cooper's knives are rare."

"I would never sell it," Jaden told them. "I watched my grandfather make that knife."

"Then it is a treasure. Thanks for helping us today. You have a very interesting shop."

"You're welcome. Have a nice visit," Jaden said as they left.

When the door closed she added, "I am so glad that knife is gone."

"I almost thought he might buy a sword," Hal commented. "He seemed knowledgeable about knives and swords. Speaking of swords, I know you have an open invitation to the Bartlett home in Big Sur to see and possibly buy Captain Josiah Bartlett's sword. That house has quite a reputation in California history. I understand it was built over a network of caves on the Big Sur cliffs especially for smuggling. It's almost the last building in the area. Nothing for miles. Then San Simeon and the road up to Hearst's Castle."

"Captain Josiah built the house there deliberately to be away from people. Bobbi is dying to see the estate. She's a California history buff. If we go, it will be after the holidays. I doubt that the expense of the sword can be justified. It would just be sitting in the case maybe for years. I plan to go just to see the home. I've never been into Big Sur anyway and I know the scenery is spectacular."

To her surprise, Bill appeared in the doorway.

"How are you feeling, Jaden?" He was dressed casually in levis and a navy blue pullover fleece sweatshirt. "I hope you are getting your energy back. Should you be working so soon?"

"Working keeps my mind off what happened, Bill. Some days I feel like I've just run the Big Sur Marathon. There's no energy at all."

"She gets better every day," Hal said.

"Have you been out much?" Bill asked.

"No," she admitted. For a few days she was even afraid to leave her apartment.

"Would you like to take a short walk down to Carmel Beach?"

"Oh, Bill, this is the first day I've come down to the shop."

Hal said, "Jaden, Bill's right. A walk in the fresh air will be wonderful for you. I think I can handle this crowd."

"All right. Yes, I'll go. Just let me get my jacket. It's cool out."

Bill smiled.

Jaden rushed back from taking her jacket from the small office under the staircase.

"Hal," Bill said as he opened the door for Jaden, "We may be awhile."

"Fine with me, Bill. You and Jaden take as long as you want."

After the door to the shop closed Hal slammed his hand down on the black velvet covered board that he used to show knives to their best advantage. He smiled and said, "Yes!"

Slash and Turn

THE SWORD OF SMUGGLERS POINT

Barbara Chamberlain

Jaden Steele slowed her antique Chevy as she approached the turn-off to Smuggler's Point Road off Highway 1 in the rugged California area called Big Sur.

Her friend, Bobbi Jones, said, "We've gone thirty miles from the intersection at Rio Road. Should be coming to Smuggler's Point. Look at those cliffs shearing down to the ocean. I can see why people love this area, but I'll bet the electricity goes out a lot in the winter." She suddenly pointed to a massive oak dripping with Spanish moss and frosted with fog.

"There it is—the famous twisted limb on that ancient oak. They say that in a storm Captain Josiah

Bartlett's ghost appears hanging and twisting from that tortured branch. He swore to stay right here until he was proved innocent of his wife's disappearance and murder."

Jaden shivered as the spirit of Josiah no doubt haunted the place where he was killed. "He swore he was innocent. He insisted that he loved his wife. Her body was never found. Bobbi, does that seem strange to you? Maybe he threw her in the ocean."

"Hung by his own father-in-law, Don Fernando Martinez, and some of his vaqueros on a stormy night. Flashes of lightning hit the ground close to the tree after the hanging. Since lightning is not common in California storms, the men were afraid to cut him down. He was twisting from the branch until the storm ended. The next morning some of his servants cut him down with his own sword, the sword we are going to see, and buried him in the family plot on the estate grounds. Isn't that a great story? And to think you have a chance to buy old Josiah's sword!" When Bobbi talked about the old California legends, she gestured with her hands. The more excited she was about the subject, the more her hands talked.

"Hal's checking on what the retail value might be. If Mr. Bartlett wants too much for it compared to the resale, I can't take the chance."

Jaden watched her finances with the same tenacity as her neighbor's cat, Arizona, might guard a captured mouse. "People would come into the store just to see that sword. Josiah Bartlett is one of the most fascinating legends of California history. I'm sure it would draw customers."

Jaden turned the car onto the fog shrouded road. "Why on earth was this place built in such a remote spot? David Bartlett told me that it was a mile from Highway 1 to the wall of the estate. It must be right on the cliff."

"Smuggler's Point should explain it, Jaden. The ship came near to the cliffs, put off a boat with the contraband, and somehow brought the merchandise from the cliffs into the basement of the house. There are networks of caves along the cliffs. The house is built over one of those networks. They say David Bartlett's grandfather made a fortune bringing in rum during prohibition. But before that there was always money to be made smuggling some contraband."

The car bumped down what was now a one lane road. "I hope the sword is worth this trip. When David Bartlett responded to my email last November, I was really surprised. I told him that we had a display case of swords. And I did not promise to buy. He still invited me for the week end."

"It's supposed to be gorgeous. A gold-plated handle set with turquoise. Captain Josiah liked the best of everything. The house is full of antiques brought from around the world and Tiffany lamps and a custom made Tiffany stained glass window at the top of the stairway. It's a stylized stained glass portrait of his wife, Rosalba. I can't wait to see the house. When you told me that David Bartlett had invited you here, I could not believe how lucky we are. And he said to bring a friend. Do you know how many people would give anything to see one of the most famous houses in California history?"

Through the mist Jaden saw the seven foot high stone wall that had protected the estate from the curious since 1850.

"David Bartlett said to press the button on the right side of the gate. He will let us in." She idled the car.

"O.K." Bobbi slipped out of the passenger's seat to disappear in the fog until she magically reappeared on the right side of the solid, weather beaten wooden plank door.

When the door opened Jaden heard the crash of waves on the Big Sur rocks below the steep cliffs.

Bobbi found the buzzer. In about thirty seconds the door creaked open.

Her friend slipped back into the passenger seat. "That creaking door is announcing a haunted house, don't you think?"

Jaden should have laughed. Something made that impossible. Could be that hangings were not a laughing matter. She drove forward slowly.

The morning fog was peppered with holes now as the sun struggled to break through to the cliffs.

A spired Victorian house appeared out of the dissipating mist like a conjurer's trick.

Jaden gasped. "Look!"

Bobbi pointed. "The ship's carpenters copied the New England homes. There's the tower or copula, where they say that Josiah Bartlett kept his wife prisoner."

"Who is they?"

"Legends. Old legends of the Big Sur coast. Josiah chased her and brought her home. The only place he could keep her was that room. Josiah was not a pillar of society. He married Roslba Martinez to gain some of her father's property as a dowry. She gave him one son. When old Josiah left for his long voyages, Rosalba hated staying on this lonely point alone."

"I don't blame her. What a lonely spot for a woman." Jaden braked her car in front of what was built as a carriage house. "There are three cars. That means civilization."

Even though they were still in the car the crash of waves on the rocky cliffs below the house drowned out her last words.

When she got out of the car the waves crashed in surround sound. The breeze blew her dark hair everywhere. She should not have even combed it this morning. The damp air would make her naturally wavy hair curl into wild ringlets. Bobbi pointed to the steps to the house that were diagonally across the asphalt pavement from them.

When they were at the bottom of the steps the door to the house opened. A woman stood in the doorway. "Jaden Steele?"

"Yes," Jaden answered as she and Bobbi walked up the six steps to the house.

They walked up into a large kitchen about the size of one of their upstairs apartments on Dolores Court in Carmel.

"Welcome to the Bartletts. So nice of you to drive all the way down here from Carmel." The tall woman extended her hand. "I'm Martha Sullivan."

The large kitchen, probably fifteen by fifteen feet, had a fireplace big enough to stand in on the wall opposite the door.

"This is my friend, Roberta Jones."

For a second Martha's face registered surprise. She frowned briefly, as though she were trying to remember, then smiled broadly. "Welcome again. We are always pleased to have visitors. Obviously we don't get many. Would you like some tea or coffee?"

Bless you, Jaden spoke silently. Aloud she said, "That would be great. Coffee, please. Black."

"And the same for me, Martha. Thank you."

"Mr. Bartlett is on the phone and will be down in a few minutes." She walked over to a six burner electric stove, picked up a red tea kettle, and filled it at the sink.

"The coffee is already made. The tea is for Mr. Bartlett," she explained, opening a door to their right. It looked like a pantry.

A cold draft that came from the storeroom made Jaden shiver.

Surprise must have showed on her face.

"It's cool for a reason," Martha explained. There's another door that leads to the wine cellar and basement."

Bobbi obviously could not resist, "Is that the way the smuggled goods were brought in?"

Martha smiled and nodded. "Yes. No one knows exactly how. There's a networks of caves through all these cliffs. When Mr. Bartlett's grandfather died, no one's ever bothered to go explore down there. It's dangerous."

"Martha?" A man's voice asked from the door. Because the light behind him made a dark shadow, Jaden squinted to see. He walked a little more into the room.

Both Jaden and Bobbi gasped at once. For a few seconds, Jaden thought the man was Bill Amirkhanian, their neighbor who lived in number three of the upstairs Dolores Court apartments in Carmel. Bill was a Carmel Police Sergeant and a well-known artist.

"I'm sorry," David Bartlett stepped into the room. "I did not mean to startle you."

Bobbi stumbled over her words. "It wasn't that, Mr. Bartlett. Just a trick of the light, I think. You look like a friend of ours. Of course we knew he could not be here."

"Yes," Jaden agreed, staring at the man. Of course he was not Bill. He could easily be a brother. The dark hair and olive complexion came from his Spanish ancestry.

Bill's came from his middle-eastern ancestors. Their physiques were similar and they both moved in the same way.

Her imagination was playing tricks or she was so attracted to Bill that she imagined the resemblance. She had already been honest enough with herself to realize that she was afraid of commitment because her first relationship with a man after her husband died was a disaster.

Sergio Panetti skipped one important detail in his life; the fact that he was married. He was murdered with a knife from her store. People had seen them arguing because Jaden was furious when she found out he was married. She became the first suspect. Bobbi became the second suspect.

"Welcome to the Bartlett House and to Smuggler's Point," David Bartlett said. "Martha is going to show you your rooms and then, if you feel like it, I can take you on a tour of the house."

Jaden wondered if they were so used to the crash of the ocean waves that they did not hear them. In her own apartment she heard the ocean often. Not always, though the waves were always there. You get used to repeated sounds.

"Your tea is ready, Mr. Bartlett," Martha poured a steaming brew into his mug.

"Thank you, Martha." He sat down at the table with them, his large hands cupping the mug. "Did you have a good trip down? How were the directions? It's a remote spot, I know."

"The drive is beautiful. I've never been to Big Sur before. I just moved to Carmel two years ago."

"And how about you, Bobbi?" David asked.

"I have been to Big Sur, but not this far down."

"Then I know you will enjoy this visit."

The unexpected crash of a wave outside caused a draft on Jaden's back. She shivered.

Look for the third book in the Jaden Steele Mystery Series,

The Sword of Smuggler's Point that will be released in 2013.

If you love a mystery, you will love how Jaden Steele solves her first cold case.

ABOUT THE AUTHOR

Barbara Chamberlain's first in the Jaden Steele Mystery Series set in Carmel, California, is receiving excellent reviews. While working in Carmel the idea for "The Jaden Steele Mysteries" began to develop. She conceived the characters on walks through the village. *A Slice of Carmel* is the first with heroine Jaden Steele. Jaden buys a cutlery store in the tourist village and forms friendships with her neighbors who live in the upstairs Dolores Court apartments. When she and librarian Bobbi Jones are accused of murder, they must team up to solve the case. Barbara has been interviewed on KSCO radio in Santa Cruz about the mysteries.

Her short story, Mall Santa, was just published in *A Miracle Under the Christmas Tree,* editor Jennifer Sanders, Harlequin. The Arkansas 2011 Writer's conference awarded her first place for her fantasy novel, The Flight of Alpha I. Her first novels, Ride the West Wind and The Prisoner's Sword, were reprinted in 2011. They were named Recommended Reading by the National Council of Teachers of English. In 2009 Barbara's original fable set in Okinawa won First Place in the Writer's

Digest Writing Competition and was published in an anthology. Her short story won first place in the Northern California Pen Women 2011 literary contest. She has published numerous short stories.

Barbara has taught storytelling and creative writing classes through adult schools and community college. At a large family genealogy conference in 2009 she facilitated a session, Telling Your Own Stories; Magic Through Memories. This was similar to a presentation done in 2007 at the NSN Sig Pre-Conference session as well as the Asilomar Reading conference in Pacific Grove. Performances have been at private parties, local organizations, the Monterey City Library's Tellabration, and the Palo Alto Children's Library Storytelling Festival. Rockin' Folktales is Barbara's CD of middle Eastern stories.

As an elementary school librarian she set up three different libraries. Barbara also worked in youth services and reference at Monterey City Library and Harrison Memorial Library in Carmel.

The University of California at Santa Cruz awarded Barbara a bachelor's degree in history. She received her Master's degree in Library and Information Science from San Jose University.

Currently, she serves as president of the Northern California Pen Women and is a member of the Santa Clara County Branch. She is a past president of the local Cabrillo Host Lions. Barbara and her husband, Dave, live in Aptos, California.